Cloaking His

By

Geoff Chandler

www.publishnation.co.uk

PROLOGUE

We enter the central character's life which, for a short time, is played out in Wichita, U.S.A. Then, leading up to this point we follow the events of his life in England one year earlier.

Peter North, the ex-British Armed Forces officer who had been dismissed from the Forces for fraudulent activities along with a psychological assessment of proven post-traumatic stress disorder which has left him with a dark side to his personality also has a criminal record for assault. These issues become problematic for him when interviewing for a job let alone hold one down.

Attending the funeral service of an ex-Armed Forces colleague North recognises the celebrant, officiating over the proceedings, to be an old acquaintance of his, Guy Williams. They make arrangements to meet.

North learns from this meeting that, being an excellent orator, he too could put himself forward as a funeral celebrant, a role for which it is not necessary to undergo any formal training, as some are led to believe. But most importantly and to North's advantage, no criminal checks are requested by the funeral directors who would take him on, and because no official vetting is required for celebrants as there is for carers, school teachers, police and the prison service who also work with the vulnerable, this is in his favour. He accompanies funeral celebrant Guy Williams on some prearranged home visits to the bereaved and to a few funeral services in order to get a handle on what to expect. For North the position of funeral celebrant would be ideal, cloaking the darkness within him and allowing it to surface.

North seizes this opportunity with both hands only to find he has to navigate a path through the contradictory needs of a Human Trafficking unit, Cold Case Fraud unit and an unscrupulous Private Detective.

1

Chapter 1

'This should never have happened, should never have come to this. You, alone with that creep, Christ, the thought of him makes my skin crawl.'

'Well, let me tell you something, that so called creep, as you so politely call him, helped me a damn sight more than you ever did at a time when I needed your help and support, and you can't say you didn't have the opportunity, hindsight is an amazing thing. But then, just like always you're full of lame excuses. One of the meanest things you ever did was not being here during his visits, after all,' she says sarcastically, 'it was only to talk through the arrangements for your father's funeral service for Christ's sake! You, you should be ashamed of yourself.'

Sinclair stands up from where they both sit. Moving his big frame in an agitated manner and drawing heavily upon his cigarette, he walks to and fro across the boards of the veranda. He stops and faces her.

'Look Mother, you know I'm under pressure what with my work load and bullshit family matters, add that to the major falling-out I had with Dad, well, I just…'

'Oh sure, the truth is,' her voice falters, 'you couldn't swallow your pride to come and see him, to make amends. For Christ's sake Sinclair, he, was, your, father! He was dying! He asked for you, you know. I saw the disappointment in his eyes 'cos he knew, yes he knew deep down you weren't coming, it was heart breaking to witness.'

Tears start to well up in her eyes as she stands and gathers up the newspapers that lay on the rattan wicker table, a family heirloom since 1850. She makes her way along the well-worn silver maple wooden veranda into the large kitchen of the family

2

ranch house where she had lived for the past 40 years since marrying farmer James Hopper Junior who in turn had inherited it from his father James Hopper.

She stands, staring out of the half-opened window that sits just above the twin-butler kitchen sink. In deep thought she unconsciously surveys the fields of corn, their edges elongated by shadows cast against the setting sun.

Sinclair treads his cigarette into the boards then makes his way inside.

'Look, mother, walking away is not going to solve anything, and anyway, this isn't about me being a complete ass-hole it's about what happened to you. And I swear to God, had I'd known dad had asked for me, well, I would have…'

'No Sinclair stop there,' she says defiantly. 'It makes no difference what you wish you had done and whatever you're about to say I'm not interested, it makes no difference and won't change a damn thing.'

'Well, if that's how you see it,' he says apathetically. 'anyways Mother, I am concerned about your wellbeing you know what with all that's happened.'

'My wellbeing you're saying, my wellbeing,' she laughs out loud. 'I'm sorry but coming from you that's got to be a damn joke, right. You're not here because of my damn wellbeing, oh no, it's to rub my face in it, in the fact that I've lost your inheritance and don't you dare say otherwise.'

'Look, you do realise that all this chaos falls on your shoulders don't you, think about it Mother. Why, Dad, his father and his father before him built this place from scratch and there you go giving it all away. I still can't take it in it's a nightmare, that bastard, he's nothing but vermin and vermin need shooting, putting down.'

Reeling from hearing this she slams her hands down onto the draining board and turns to face him, shouting.

'No! You stop right there, stop it,' she shakes with rage. 'I'll not have a bad word said about Peter especially the threats, you hear me.'

3

Her reaction sends him stepping back into the old large two panelled oak table that has served the family for generations. It doesn't budge.

'Bloody hell Mother will you calm down.' rubbing the backs of his legs, he says, 'you know what? I'm so fucking pissed just hearing that guy's name. It's Peter this, Peter that, for Christ's sake. Just how close were you two anyway?'

'Sorry…say again!'

He realises he shouldn't have gone so far as to say what he did but he presses on.

'You know,' he half grins. 'its text book stuff, the lonely, vulnerable woman being taken advantage of.'

'I'm not sure what you're getting at Sinclair, but if it's what I think, you need to wash that foul mouth out of yours, or would you rather me say I gave him my body and let him do what he do, and that I enjoyed every minute of it.'

'Why that's disgusting, talking like that. If dad could hear you he would…'

'Well he isn't. Just talk is it, is that what you reckon. Just you keep on guessing.'

With his father in mind he feels betrayed.

'That guy's a dead man walking.'

'What have I told you about that big mouth of yours, you will bring trouble upon yourself one of these days,' she tries to defuse some of the tension. 'the celebrant understood me, knew what I was going through, no one else did, why, you didn't, you didn't even ask how I was, how I felt and was I managing to cope. Nope, there was no one there for me except him, who by the way didn't ask for money. After having heard him talk of his aspirations in life I gladly offered it to him. The whole thing was so genuine, so refreshing to hear at a time when everything around me felt odd, lonely, hollow and deathly.'

She places the worn black handled steel kettle on top of the wood burning stove.

'But can't you see Mother, he clearly took advantage of your state of mind, you were grieving. How he got away with this sort of thing in England, 'cos I'm guessing he must have done the same to a lot of folk there, we'll never know. So why don't you

4

admit to that at least then I could go some way to understanding, you know, be well, more sympathetic.'

'Oh don't you bother, you wouldn't know the meaning of the word. I can assure you that I was and am completely compos mentis. Let me tell you something else about him, he had hope, don't you understand...hope! And if there's something been missing around here over these past years it's been fucking hope.'

Pulling opening the large fridge door she stops, lost in thought, remembering how Peter comforted her, holding her in his arms. How safe she felt and yet excited at the same time. Having regained her composure she grabs for the milk carton and slams the fridge door shut.

'I mean,' she laughs. 'look at you and your lot Sinclair it's bloody pathetic, there's no room for hope in the way you live, it's stifling, oppressive all holed up in that slick city house of yours. You and your lot just keep going round and round and round in the same old bloody circles, Christ I tell you it's depressing to watch, you lot being slowly drained of hope. If hope is the only thing that is supposed to separate us as a species, then what the fuck does that make those without it, what does it make you, what does it make me?'

The kettle rattles on the stove as the boiling water tries to keep its grip on the steam.

'Your Father's aspirations and hopes for a family reunion well,' she says with venom. 'That all went to crap years ago, you made damn sure of that.'

Using an old scorched tea towel she removes the boiling kettle from the stove then places it on a trivet, puts scoops of coffee into a pot before pouring in the steaming hot water, the aroma of coffee fills the air. She places its lid on.

'Don't Mum,' he pleads. 'Please, don't talk like that.' he holds his arms out gesturing for a hug, she raises her hands and steps back.

'No Sinclair no, don't, I can't.'

'For Christ's sake Mother, have you no compassion?'

She shouts. 'How dare you have the nerve to talk about compassion?'

5

Pulling out a screwed up pack of cigarettes and a lighter from his trouser pocket Sinclair gets ready to have a cigarette.

'You and that filthy habit, you'll never quit, because you're weak.'

'Yeah sure I am.' He says nonchalantly.

Regardless of her putdown, he lights one.

'By the way, I didn't, as you put it, sign everything away that just didn't come in to it. I lent him money, sure I did and that's all I did. I'd do it again if it would help someone's future to burn bright.'

'Just listen to yourself, for Christ's sake.' He turns the screw. 'The guy's a conman. It's as plain as that. To him you were really nothing just some lonely old fool, a bereaving woman just primed to be taken advantage of and I bet that you've not been the only one to fall under his, oh I don't know a better word for it, under his spell.'

Shocked by what he had said she slaps him across the face. He recoils in shock.

'What the hell Mother!' using a fingertip and his tongue he feels for swelling and for any blood on his lip. His fingertip is bloodied.

'You've changed mother, oh how you've changed. Look around you. Yes, you gave him money ok, but you gave him so much you haven't been able to keep the ranch from falling into dilapidation and it's soon to be repossessed by the bank. You're going to be left with nothing, nothing I tell you.'

Filled with rage she points to the door.

'Get out! Get out of this house now! Or so help me God I will…'

'The truth hurts doesn't it, can't you see, the guy has taken you for a damn fool what with his English ways and all, I swear to God, that son of a bitch is gonna regret ever setting foot through the front door, regret coming to America. he's going back to where he came from in a box.'

'Get out now, and you leave him be, for pity's fucking sake, just let him and me be.'

Before stepping out onto the veranda he stops in the doorway, silhouetted against the low sun he turns to face her.

6

'Know what Mother, in a way you're just as screwed up as he is. You both make me sick.'

Her body language telegraphs that she is about to take a run and swing at him. As she does so he grabs her wrist. She tries hard to force her hand, keeping the momentum going, but unable to match his strength, she reluctantly relents. Physically and emotionally drained she crumples, dropping down on to her hands and knees, her head hanging low to the floor and sobbing uncontrollably.

Sinclair seizes this opportunity and quickly takes a weapon and a ammo clip from the gun case that's kept inside one of the kitchen units. He holds the gun and ammo clip hidden behind his back.

Scornfully, he looks down at her.

'Some Mother you are.'

With the aid of a kitchen stool she manages to pull herself up and then with every sinew left within her she feebly pushes against him trying to get him to leave.

'Ok, ok, ok for fucks sake, I'm going. You know what, what that celebrant took from you he took from us all, the family. He just can't get away with doing what he's done.'

Sinclair jumps down the five steps of the veranda that lead to the driveway. She is left exhausted, leaning against the doorframe.

He shouts 'I'm going to do what Dad would have done and that's to teach that son of a bitch a lesson.'

She turns her back on him goes inside and slams the door shut, leaning with her back against it she slowly slides down into a squatting position and buries her head in her hands.

Before reaching his red 1964 Mustang 2+2 Fastback, he calls out to her.

'Oh and by the way I thought you had better know, I've made enquiries, happens to be that, that son of a bitch will be taking old Mr Bill Cartwright's funeral service at the crematorium tomorrow and I'll be there making damn sure it's Peter fucking North's last funeral service that he's ever gonna give.'

The Mustang kicks up a trail of orange-tinged dust as it speeds away.

Chapter 2

In the heat of the afternoon, inside an uncomfortably hot church, situated in a suburb of Wichita, celebrant Peter North, wearing a top of the range Armani suit, stands at the lectern preparing to address mourners for the funeral service of the late Mr Bill Cartwright, a ranch worker from one of the biggest ranches in the area.

Most mourners sit, rapidly wafting their folding fans in an attempt to keep cool, others use loose hymn sheets. Young children are becoming restless, some leaning forward from where they sit, reaching out and grabbing at the hymn books and hymn sheets that are slotted into the back of the pews in front of them. The occasional child runs amok between the aisles and whispered threats can be heard from their parents letting them know they must behave, or else. Some parents sit either side, like bookends, constraining their struggling offspring who also want to take part in all the fun. On the front pew sits the widow Mrs Peggy Cartwright who is being fanned and comforted by her daughter Rose-lea.

Familiarising himself with the service notes, in preparation for the start of the funeral service, Peter North notices movement in his peripheral vision as a figure steps forward approaching from the left of the lectern.

Slowly raising his eyes up from his notes, North finds himself looking down the wrong end of the barrel of a Smith and Weston 45 Colt Double-Action firearm.

As it dawns on the congregation what's taking place, the sound of gasps and cries of children fill the chapel.

Standing in front of North and nervously brandishing a firearm stands a fair headed, overweight, above average sized male, the cut of his clothes more suited for a city-slicker than those one would wear for a ranch hand's funeral service.

North thinks what the fuck! 'Look brother, what's this all about, I'm about to conduct a funeral service here.'

Adrenalin is rushing through the assailant's veins. His heart rate is sky-high and he is breathing heavily, sweating profusely and is unable to stop his outstretched arm, that's holding the firearm, from shaking.

'Don't you dare move Mr Peter North.'

To gain the mourners full attention the assailant glances over his shoulder at them and frantically waves his free arm signalling them to remain seated. Some have already managed to leave by slipping out of one of the opened side doors of the chapel.

'Quieten down and remain seated! Everyone, you all quieten down now, and listen up.'

'Please brother,' North speaks calmly. 'I don't know what you expect to achieve by doing this but there are people here mourning their loss. There are children here too.'

'Don't you dare call me the fuck your brother or so help me God I will …. It doesn't matter to me if I blow your brains out now, in five or in ten minutes time. I really don't mind,' his mouth is dry, finding it difficult to speak. 'But it's no good you getting shot dead and not knowing the reason why. Why Hell no.'

North is momentarily transported back to the horrors of the battle field. He fights to clear his mind-mist and think straight. He tries to catch a glimpse of the weapons safety catch. Is it on or off, on will give him that extra split second he needs to act.

The assailant positions himself sideways on, half facing the mourners and half facing North, quickly, frequently glancing back and forth.

'Folks this son of a bitch here, yes this devil who has been made welcome by y'all, who we have invited into our homes and let eat at our tables is a fraud, maybe worse, you all don't know, I do.'

North's combat training, survival instincts kick in. Second nature to him is attack rather than defence and that no matter how mundane an object is, it can be used as a weapon. His thoughts turn to the lectern, but it's secured to the floor. He considers his pen and his keys, dangerous in the right hands.

'Folks this Godforsaken thing standing in front of you has ruined my mother's life, my family's life too.'

North can now tell that the safety catch on the weapon is on. He thinks, now who the hell is this woman he's on about, could try talking him down but to do that I need to be certain of which woman he means, which bloody woman, there's been so many.

'No doubt people there are others amongst y'all who have suffered at this Devil's fraudulent hands. I'm not one to blame you, for he is the Devil. There are those amongst us, no doubt, too ashamed of coming forward, to speak out about what he has inflicted on them. They know what I'm talking about, his foul and fraudulent ways and more I guess.'

North starts to think clearly, I'm counting the seconds every time you look away fella. Just the one distraction, that'll be my cue. Unseen, he slowly moves his hand across his notes for his Montegrappa top of the range fountain pen, which will become a weapon in his hand.

'Well preacher! Celebrant or what the hell ya call yourself, why, you're not even Godly like. You say you only officiate at non-religious funeral services! I mean, what the hell is that all about!' North takes hold of the pen. 'You folk, listen up now, you've got to wonder what happened in England to make this asshole come all the way over here. Come on now, don't it make you wonder, it do me. This here big-shot Mr Peter North took advantage of my Mother, Mrs Bertha Hopper, y'all may know her, and who, due to his evil fraudulent ways, is about to lose everything she has.'

Sirens can be heard wailing in the distance from an approaching S.W.A.T team.

North thinks, of course, now I know which woman this guy's on about. So this is the fucking son of a bitch she talked about. Now what's this bastard's name?'

'So, in the sight of God and all these here witnesses I'm putting an end to your evil ways, It stops right here, right now! Mr fucking celebrant.'

North suddenly remembers his name.

'You're Sinclair right?'

Sinclair is taken aback at hearing this, 'Shut your mouth. Shut your fucking mouth Mr.'

'Listen Sinclair you don't have to do this, think about your Mother.'

'I said, shut, your, fucking, mouth and don't you dare mention my mother again.'

Sinclair attempts to steady his aim by clutching the revolver's hand grip with both hands. As if one, the congregation take a sharp intake of breath, some look away, some bury their faces into the arms of those sitting next to them, some are frozen to the spot with fear, unable to move due to the incomprehensibility of the situation, some cover the ears and eyes of crying children.

North has decided to make his move and move fast when outside the chapel vehicles with their sirens blaring, can be heard screeching to a halt. The chapel doors tentatively open as the S.W.A.T team, weapons drawn, ease their way into position. Sinclair is distracted. Captain O'Neil of the S.W.A.T team calls out a command.

'Police Sir! Put the weapon down and back off.'

North, still fired up , ready to make his move puts his plan of action on hold.

On hearing the command, Sinclair quickly turns, looking towards the direction the voice came from, then faces back to North who is looking past him over his shoulder.

'No, no, you look at me you son of a bitch not them, me.'

Sinclair releases the safety catch. North is impressed.

North had seen the look on Sinclair's face before. It was a look that said he was prepared to kill. A look he had seen many times in the heat of battle.

'Sir, I'm Captain O'Neil, put the weapon down and step back, now! That is an order.'

Police officers usher out the few mourners who are cowering behind the pews at the back of the chapel.

'This is your final warning, place your weapon down and move away.'

11

Captain O'Neil signals an order, members of the S.W.A.T team stealthily move closer.

Sinclair is now in a state of uncontrollable sobbing, tears blurring his vision. He steadies his aim once more at North. He shouts out.

'This is for you Mother.... it's for you.'

Meanwhile a police marksman, at the rear of the chapel has had Sinclair in his sights. Slowly sliding his index finger onto the trigger he waits for the order in his earpiece to take the man down.

'Sir stop, your mother called us, a Mrs Bertha Hopper, she's told us everything.'

'My mother told you?'

With his sleeve he wipes the tears and sweat from his eyes.

'Yes everything. You are bound to be upset by it all, but we can work this out. Look, can I call you Sinclair,' he doesn't answer. 'Sinclair, just place your weapon down and step back, everything will be ok. We've sent a patrol car to bring your mother here'

'She's coming here? Oh no, why for Christ's sake. Why?'

He lowers the weapon to his side. North can barely control his urge to act.

'She's under this devil's spell, he controls her, don't listen to her, she's confused.'

North thinks, that's it, this has gone far enough. Pen in one hand he athletically hurls himself over the lectern and, with his free hand he grabs hold of Sinclair's arm, directing the aim of fire away. North sends Sinclair falling backwards into the aisle and lands on top of him with a thud, both narrowly missing the now even more distraught Mrs Cartwright and her daughter, who are dragged away to safety by a family member.

The impact from their fall forces the firearm out of Sinclair's grip it then slides under one of the pews, out of reach of both of them. Now, laying on the floor and heavily winded from the fall, both men start to struggle with one another. North tries to weaken Sinclair by repeatedly stabbing at him anywhere he can with the sharp fountainpen, eventually it snaps. They continue exchanging punches and kicks as they roll in the aisle,

12

pulling and climbing over each other in their attempt to be the first to reach the firearm. Gunshots ring out as two bullets are discharged from the firearm, one ricocheting off the walls of the chapel before coming to rest with a loud thud as it embeds itself in one of the large oak roof beams.

Mayhem ensues as the rest of the mourners are rushed out of the chapel under the direction of police officers. The S.W.A.T. Team move in closer.

Flashes of red laser spots from their weapons dance and bounce off the dark oak pews before coming to rest on the two male bodies that now lay, still, entangled, on the floor of the chapel. Breathing heavily and groaning with pain, one of the two men eventually releases himself from the clutches of the other. The firearm falls in between them on to the floor. Captain O'Neil moves in, weapon drawn.

'Stay still and do not move. I repeat, do not move. If you do, you will be shot. You, will, be, shot. Do you understand?'

At that point the firearm is kicked away, out of reach, by an officer who had made her way forward by jumping over the back of the pews.

Captain O'Neil stands astride one of the bloodied men, who is laying on his side and looking up at him and finding it hard to catch a breath. Captain O'Neil barks an order at him.

'Roll over, face down and place both your hands behind your back. Now!'

Captain O'Neil holsters his weapon, kneels down on one knee and places a set of handcuffs around the bloodied wrists. Then, by grabbing him under both arms, O'Neil pulls the man up to the kneeling position. The other man lies bloodied and motionless, an officer checks for signs of life…..

'Captain O'Neil, Sir this one's dead.'

Chapter 3

Eleven months earlier.
Portsmouth Crematorium. England.

Inside the South Chapel of Portsmouth Crematorium a funeral service is about to take place, mourners await the start of the service which is to be officiated by the celebrant Peter North.

On top of the polished dark oak lectern at which he stands, are North's service notes and a small microphone. Embedded in the top right hand corner of the lectern are three discreet buttons, one coloured green is labelled music, one coloured amber is labelled 'music fade', and finally, a red button labelled 'curtains closed'. Stapled to the bottom left hand corner of the lectern is a small, but polite reminder to the orator, of the crematorium's rules and underlined, in bold red, are the words: Do not go over the allotted time of 40 minutes.

To signal the service is about to begin, North thumbs over the first page of the service notes then looks up and faces the mourners; he discreetly presses the amber button and whilst the introductory music 'Amazing Grace' slowly fades to silence North calculates that there are at least 65 mourners attending the service, the capacity of the chapel is 200. 50 of the 65 mourners to his reckoning must be hitting the grand old age of 80 plus and 12 others are obviously assigned carers who have travelled with the oldies from various care homes. The remaining 3 women, who are wearing different elaborate styles of fascinators and sunglasses, look like they're from the cast of Desperate Housewives and though obviously friends of the Zara Maxwell the widow do not seem too bothered at being here.

North goes on to think, the oldies have made a huge fucking effort to be here paying their last respects to the old man, so

14

good on them, and as for the widow, the sexy young Mrs Maxwell, well, looks like she could have had something to do with shortening the old man's life expectancy, the lucky bastard.

He pauses for a few seconds, before speaking over the small microphone, in a relaxed and meaningful manner but loud enough so that the hard of hearing, probably most of the congregation, can keep up.

Beginning with the well-rehearsed opening lines that he has used on many such occasions, the only difference is the name of the deceased.

'Welcome, welcome here today as we join together in loving memory of Mr Donald James Maxwell. My name is Peter, Peter North and I am your officiant today. I would like to take this opportunity to once again offer my sincere condolences to Donald's wife Zara whom I met with earlier.' There are giggles from the three women. 'I also offer my condolences to all family members and friends. Indeed to all at this time of loss. It is an impossibility to encapsulate the whole life essence of Donald, his love, his joys of life in words alone.' There is whispering and even more giggling coming from the three women. North thinks, you fucking assholes. 'So today as we share but a glimpse into Donald's life, we remember how he touched our lives and how we in turn touched his.' One of the three women sniggers.

North has had enough. He stops speaking, his body language and facial expression, clearly showing his displeasure and annoyance due to their antics. There is an uncomfortable silence in the chapel as the three women fidget in their seats trying to gain some composure.

'Ladies,' North stares at them. 'can we show some dignity and respect please, thank you.' He feels like the least he could do is to throttle them all.

He continues with the introduction. 'I am sure that in times of reflection whether it is with family members, friends or in times of private reflection, further endearing memories of Donald will come to mind.' He clears his throat. 'And so began the life of Donald James Maxwell...'

Scarred by the trauma of the conflicts of war, in Peter North lies a darkness which has left him devoid of all faith in the human race and in the Gods, but then he had none to begin with. Since leaving the military he has spent the occasional night in police cells and worked dead-end jobs. Now, ironically, he works as a celebrant officiating at non-religious funeral services. A position in which North manipulates and takes advantage of the bereaved whilst knowing that due to his victims' gullibility and shame, they are unwilling to speak out.

As the service approaches its end, he discreetly presses the red button, signalling to those behind the scene to start the heavy, dark crimson curtains in motion. After a short pause the curtains begin to slowly close around the plinth on which the coffin lays, and as they do so, North speaks some parting words of comfort, words that he had spoken many times before.

'So let us keep in our hearts the memories of the love and joy that Donald brought into our lives and may his love stay in our hearts forever. It has been an honour for me to have officiated over Donald Maxwell's service. I thank you.'

As the music 'Angel' by Robbie Williams filters its way through the speakers, the mourners, starting from the front of the chapel, are lead out by Funeral Director James Clifton of J.C. Funeral Services. Once outside the chapel the big oak doors slowly close silently behind them.

Funeral Director James Clifton re-enters the chapel and hands over a sealed envelope to North containing his fee. Without the need to count it he slips the envelope into his trouser pocket.

'Thanks James.'

'No, thank you my dear man. How rude those obnoxious women were, I mean I could even hear them sniggering from the back of the chapel. It's the youth of today I'm afraid, but you handled it very well I must say. A put down or two doesn't harm anyone and boy did those three need putting down a peg or two. Peter, Ruth will be in contact with you shortly regarding another service, but for now I must fly, bye Peter love.'

After all this time North still feels uncomfortable being called love by James Clifton but then he laughs to himself, thinking, who else would have the balls to say that to me. Apart from the sounds coming from behind the heavy curtains as the crematorium porters remove the coffin from the plinth, all is deathly quiet. North stands alone as he often does remembering fallen comrades. He gathers up his notes and slips them into a slim black briefcase. Before stepping down from the lectern he adjusts his tie and runs his fingers through his hair. He picks up the briefcase and, taking a deep breath, he mentally prepares himself to meet the mourners who are now gathered outside the chapel.

North sees that 32 year old widow Zara Maxwell, wearing a Stella McCartney Nicole velvet jacket, is crouched down, with other mourners, predominantly women, reading and remarking on the cards of sympathy and remembrance that are attached to the splendid floral displays laid out before them.

North makes his way towards her, but to his annoyance, his progress is hindered by family members and friends of the deceased Donald Maxwell wanting to congratulate him on the way he conducted the funeral service. Uninterested in what they have to say he half-heartedly chats to them, politely edging himself away, closing in on Zara Maxwell.

North thinks, I must get her on her own before she decides to leave.

Navigating a clear route through the mourners, some in wheel chairs with their carers, he continues towards her.

One of the three friends of Zara Maxwell sees him approaching and whispers to her. 'Zara, that good-looking celebrant is coming over. Put in a good word for me will you, he's so gorgeous!'

'Lisa Forrester, you are terrible…..but you're right! He's gorgeous.'

Zara Maxwell stands, readjusts her clothing and greets him.

'Peter thank you so much. That was a lovely service.'

She gives him a hug. He can't help noticing how good she smells.

'Thank you Zara.' North needs to get her alone to further carry out his plan.

'Zara, let's stroll for a while, the Garden of Remembrance is beautiful this time of year.'

He has caught the unwanted attention of the three friends who are stood eyeing him up and whispering to one another. He thinks, disrespectful bitches.

'Excuse us ladies.' It pisses him off to be polite to them. 'Don't worry I will take good care of her I promise!' He thinks so in the meantime go fuck your selves.

North slowly guides Zara away out of the earshot of the mourners who are busying themselves chatting to one another and continuing to admire the flora.

'So Zara, while I have you to myself.'

He thinks, at bloody last.

'May I ask, have you thought of how you're going to move forward from here on in?'

'Well I just have no idea. But I guess I would like to eventually meet someone like, well, someone like you, who would make me feel appreciated and cared for as you have during your visits and phone calls over these past few weeks. Family and friends haven't been able to do that, but somehow you have. It's been amazing really.'

He thinks, this is all too easy, like taking candy from a baby comes to mind.

'Thank you Zara, why, that's high praise indeed. During my visits I felt there was a connection between us, now I hope you don't mind me saying that?'

He thinks, of course she doesn't she loves it. All the signs have been there since day one.

North makes sure she feels his presence by edging closer to her but not too close, not too dominating. He thinks, easy does it.

'No Peter, if anything, I'm relieved to hear you say that. Terrible of me I know, and under such circumstances too. Whatever must you think of me?' He remains silent, his training has taught him that by remaining silent the interrogated give more information than they intend to. 'As I told you, these

18

last years have not been good years for me living with a man more than twice my age, in actual fact you were a light in all the darkness, and yet I know nothing about you, but in a way I feel I do, Christ does that make sense? I looked forward to your visits when you were so focused on me. That made me feel wanted but how could I have admitted that to you in this situation.'

He can't get his mind off of just how great her body looks.

'You know that you can talk to me about anything Zara and it won't go any further, strictly between you and me.'

They continue with their walk in the Garden of Remembrance. North constantly gauging the situation, interjecting conversation when and where needed to keep things bordering on a level of interest yet with a hint of tease and innuendo.

'Zara, I must say, you look stunning just as you did during my visits, by the way what's the perfume?'

'It's my own personal formula, I just love it.'

'You should market it.'

'That's nice of you to say.'

'To my reckoning Zara you must be the sweetest smelling flower in this garden.'

He thinks, sweet smelling flower, I can't believe I said that shit, she'll throw up in a minute.

Zara giggles. He's reminded of the three bitches in the chapel.

He says. 'Without me sounding too presumptuous, but if you are ever in need of that chat or even maybe stretch that to a drink, please don't hesitate to get in contact with me, in fact, to cheer you up, I insist!'

She smiles then looks up at the threatening darkening clouds. Holding out her black leather gloved hand, drops of rain begin to settle on its palm.

'Looks like it's starting to rain Peter, I guess we should be making our way back to the others. They'll be wondering where we got to.'

Not wanting to get caught out in a heavy downpour their pace quickens to where family and friends are now standing under a sea of black umbrellas, chatting amongst themselves.

Before arriving they stop and hug each other. North lightly kisses her on the cheek, then whispers. 'Call me.'

She slowly releases his hand then mouths back.

'I will.'

As Zara returns to her family and friends, North starts to walk back to where his car is parked. He takes one last look over his shoulder at her and, as he does so, he spots one of the three young women break away from the group and start running towards him, trying to catch him up.

He mutters under his breath, now, what the fuck does that bitch want. Maybe that fucking Maxwell has said something, soon find out I guess.

He looks on with a great deal of satisfaction and amusement as the wind and rain tries its best to impede her efforts and takes its toll on her expensive Alexander McQueen jacket and trousers not to mention the fascinator and sunglasses. The open umbrella is trying hard to release itself from her grasp, trying to turn itself inside out. He stops, raises his jacket collar, and waits, wondering if Zara Maxwell had also shared their private conversation with the other two.

He mutters under his breath. 'If she has said anything to them I'll fucking make her suffer.'

Wet and out of breath the windswept woman finally catches up with him.

'Hi! Peter isn't it?' She finally takes control of her umbrella. 'I was wondering if I could have a business card of yours, you never know what this life will throw at you!'

He quickly comes to the conclusion that Maxwell must have kept her mouth shut after all, a yardstick of whatever I intend to put that bitch Maxwell through now I know she'll keep shtum.

'You're right, you never do.' He thinks, I detest people like you. 'And you are?'

'Oh sorry, I'm Lisa, Lisa Forrester; I know Zara Maxwell.'

'I take it you and your two friends weren't close to the late Mr Maxwell then.'

'What, what do you mean?'

I'm referring to the lack of respect you and the other two showed during his service.'

'Well, you don't take any prisoners do you?'

Harshly he says. 'No I don't, not when it comes to people like you.'

'Sorry! What do you mean people like me?'

'The sort who goes through life trampling over people and not giving a shit.'

'I don't believe this, I...'

'Look, you just don't see it. You lot never do. I'm off. Oh by the way you've just had a psychotherapy session. No charge.'

'Why you cheeky bastard, as for in the chapel I...'

'Forget it, you're not the first and you won't be the last.'

North turns his back on her and walks away.

Dumbfounded by his verbal attack on her, she runs after him and grabs him by the arm. 'Will you just stop and hear me out.'

He stops. 'Listen lady you should be apologising to all those people back there, not me. It couldn't have been nice for them hearing the contempt for the dead that you three displayed.'

'Ok, ok, look that wasn't the real me back there, and yes you're right I should be ashamed of myself, I'm sorry, I don't know what else can I say?'

'Look, just drop it. Now what was it you wanted?'

'One of your business cards if it's still ok with you.'

In an attempt to keep himself and his briefcase dry, North struggles with his six foot frame, to find some form of shelter under her umbrella. She giggles as they both jostle for a position that would accommodate them both. Again he is reminded of her antics in the chapel. North reaches into his briefcase and produces a business card. Now they both have to shout even more to be heard above the noise of the increasing strength of the wind and rain.

'Here you go! As you can see I'm available at all times, even in this bloody weather!'

She laughs.

'Thanks Peter! And I am sorry. I'll be in contact. Got to go, don't get too wet! Bye.'

North is left standing in the pouring rain, now too wet to be bothered. He calls out, 'Ditto.'

Watching her as she makes her way back to the sea of black umbrellas, North thinks, great ass, and just what the hell was that really all about anyway. He looks up at the sky, the fast approaching bluey black clouds threaten that the heavens are about to open even more.

By the time North reaches his car he receives a voicemail notification from his mobile phone. Whilst sitting in his car and drying himself off as best as he can with paper towels he plays the voicemail on loud speaker.

'Oh dearie me, I wasn't expecting to have to leave a message! It's me Peter, Ida, Ida Summers you spoke at my husband's, Harry Summers, service only a month ago. Please call me back. Hello Peter? Oh these damn fandangle machines.'

The voicemail disconnects. North smiles as he thinks, loneliness, the need to feel wanted and the need to be useful to others in this life can be an expensive business Ida, this is going cost you.

North slowly drives towards the exit. Glancing in his rear-view mirror, he sees Joan Maxwell and entourage still standing where he had left them, congregated outside the chapel in the pouring rain.

Chapter 4

Having finished his daily early morning workout using free weights followed by a 5K run on one of the running machines and 20 lengths of the swimming pool, at Hunters, a private members health club, Peter North sits relaxing in one of the mixed sex steam rooms of the spa section. It's about the time of day when it's not busy in the spa. On occasions, he is joined by another club member. They are on first name terms and while away the time chatting to one another. Her name is Fay.

*

In the newly refurbished lounge of his local public house 'The Swan' North busies himself formulating the eulogy for his next funeral service. On his table are the remnants of a bar meal and a half drunk pint of lager. All of which are strategically placed so as not to stain his notes. An incoming call on his mobile phone interrupts him, he curses, 'for fucks sake what next?' He recognises the call to be from J.C. Funeral Services one of the many funeral directors who have him on their books as a celebrant. Tucking the mobile against his ear, he continues to tap away on his laptop and answers.

'Hello this is Peter North speaking.'

'Yes, hi Peter, it's Ruth Cumberland from J.C. Funeral Services.'

'Oh, hi Ruth, how are you?' He opens his diary in anticipation of a booking for another funeral service.

'I'm good thanks Peter, I was checking on your availability to take a service, at Portsmouth Crematorium, for the morning of the 1st of November at 9.15am?'

'Just a second Ruth while I check.'

North searches through the pages of his diary.

'Yes, that's fine I'm free.'

'*Great, I will email all the information on to you. What's it to be this time cash or cheque?*'

'*Cash please Ruth.* He thinks, fuck the Tax man. '*And like always, as soon as I have paid a visit to the family, I'll get back in touch with you regarding their choice of music and Order of Service, if they choose to have one that is.*'

'*Thanks Peter you're a star, bye for now.*'

North catches the attention of Mia, who is busy working behind the bar, by holding up his now empty beer glass, signalling for another. She acknowledges him with a smile. Having finished serving a customer she pulls a pint of lager and takes it over to him.

'It's only because you tip well I do this, you do realise that don't you Peter?' She picks up the empty glass in exchange for the full one.

'Ah, Mia my love, and there's me thinking it's because you can't resist my animal magnetism! You know you mean everything in the world to me darling.'

She sheepishly looks around the lounge to see if they have been overheard. No reaction.

'Ssh, Peter, stop it, people will hear! Anyway, I bet the boss isn't too pleased with you setting up office in here again especially since the refurb and let's not forget, having barred you twice already.'

She whispers, 'The regulars are beginning to complain again.'

He thinks, fuck the miserable old bastards.

'Look Mia.' His voice quietens. 'Don't you go worrying your pretty head about them they need to get a life, it's all been taken care of, since Big Dean last barred me I've officiated at his old man's funeral service, telling everyone how good and loving a person his old man was. Although by all accounts what I said was all a load of bollocks, his old man was a nasty little vicious fucker and everyone knew it. All he passed on in this world was an empty prison cell for the next sucker. Big Dean's sort of mellowed out since the funeral so I don't think he will be barring me again, well, not for some time anyway. I feel he wants to cleanse his sins and go to heaven! But then no, I can't imagine heaven being so desperate as to have him, he should try hell.'

'Peter, you are such a terrible man!'

Mia blows him a kiss, smiles and walks back towards the bar clearing tables of empty glasses as she goes. North eyes her all the way. He thinks, great ass.

Chapter 5

On one of Portsmouth's busy high streets, DI Fay Guilford and DS Paul Grant of the Human Exploitation and Organised Crime Command (SCD9) primarily tasked with investigating human trafficking, are parked up in their unmarked SUV and are on surveillance, covertly taking photos of those paying their last respects to the late Mr Dennis Forrester whose body is in the Chapel of Rest of J.C. Funeral Services.

DS Paul Grant thumps the palms of his hands on the steering wheel.

'Fuck! We were that bloody close to finalising our plan then Forrester goes and dies on us taking key info with him to the fucking grave. Talk about bad timing. Now there's a good chance that those women and children will become untraceable, lost in the human trafficking system, without hope. And yet, here we are, bloody well staking out a funeral parlour in the hope of finding a lead, tell me, is that desperate or what?'

'Look Paul, if there's the slightest chance of a lead and if this is what it takes, then we've got to try it.'

'Okay, true, but the window of opportunity is closing in on us fast.'

Grant starts to tap on the steering wheel with his fingers.

'For fuck sake Paul, can you just stop it, you drive me mad when you do that.'

After letting out a big sigh, he stops.

'Fay, I am so, so fucking bored. You wouldn't have guessed this but before joining the force I used to play drums in a punk stroke rock band, we had a good following. Wouldn't say we were destined for the big time but man it was fun.'

'Really! You in a punk rock band, no way, what were you called?'

'Well we thought long and hard about this at the time and came up with the name Nuts.'

Guilford burst out laughing. 'Oh yes, with a name like that you were destined for glory alright. Why the name 'Nuts' for fuck sake?'

'Guess we sounded like a load of bollocks! Well we were told we did.'

She burst out laughing again. 'I can believe that, you often talk it, a load of bollocks that is.'

Grant clears his throat.

Worryingly she says, 'Christ Paul you're not going to sing are you?'

He laughs. 'No, but listen to this.' Grant starts talking in his formal interviewing voice.

'So Mr Dennis Forrester where were you at 4.45pm on Tuesday the 26th September?'

With his best attempt at a cockney accent Grant tries to mimic the late Mr Dennis Forrester.

'I was laying low Guvnor, real low, like laid out flat in the chapel of rest, honest guv.'

'Right Paul, yes very fucking funny, you dickhead, you should have sold the drums and failed as a comedian instead. You would have had more street cred.'

'But Fay, that's what I call a fucking good alibi, solid concrete, not the bull shit Forrester fed us during 'Operation Chessboard' in which, by the way, he was more heavily involved in the human trafficking scene than he let on.'

Guilford breathes heavily, huffing on the passenger's window using her index finger she draws a random pattern in the condensation before it clears.

'Oh come on Fay you knew it, I knew it, and he knew it, it was all bull shit!'

'You've been going on and on about that for ages. It's about time you let it go.'

Guilford shuffles in her seat, using one of her shoes as leverage she slips the other one off. Lifting her leg up, she starts to massage her foot.

'Oh yes! God that feels better. You know what Paul? I'm going to book myself in for a full body massage at my health

27

club as soon as this is all over and done with, you know, release all the tension, just relax it out.'

'You mean one of those spa day things.'

'It's not exactly a spa day, it's one of the many treatments that the health club offers its members. But yes they do spa days, I've been on a few and they are fantastic.'

'It's a right waste of good money, if you ask me. Paying to lounge around and sweat, I mean what do you get out of it?'

'You tight miserable old git, nothing could be better, it's good for you and you get to meet some interesting people.'

'You can meet interesting people down at the pub.'

'You know what Paul? There's no hope for you.'

She looks at her watch and yawns.

'Well, it's getting late, I'm dog tired, my bloody ass feels completely numb and my feet are killing me due to the lack of a good blood supply, I suppose that's what you get for being crouched up in this burger and coffee smelling rubbish tip of a car of yours and, just like yesterday there's been no action here.'

She checks her watch again.

'Old J.C.'s about to shut up shop, let's get back to base, I'll call it in.'

Guilford places the digital camera with its auto focus lens in the glove compartment and reaches for her seatbelt. Grant readies himself in the driver's seat. As the SUV's engine kicks into life Grant suddenly has a change of mind and cuts the engine dead.

'What's up? Come on Paul let's get going. I'm in need of a shower I must stink to high heaven.'

'No wait! Give me a minute will you, we need to speed things up a bit here. I'm just going to shoot across, try and catch them before they close.'

Grant releases his seatbelt, opens the door and starts to get out. Guilford grabs his left arm.

'No Paul! Bloody hell, get the fuck back in! What do you think you're doing man? You'll blow our cover.'

Grant jerks his arm away from her grip.

'Look I'm going.'

'No, you're fucking not. Now I'm pulling rank on you DS Grant and ordering you to remain in this vehicle.'

Ignoring Guilford's order, Grant exits the car, slams the door shut and begins weaving through the heavy traffic as he makes his way across the busy high street to J.C. Funeral Services.

Chapter 6

The noise from the hustle and bustle of the high street disappears as soon as Grant enters the premises and closes the door behind him.

The large reception area is adorned with a variety of flowers. In the background classical music can be heard playing. Before he has a chance to reach the reception desk, a tall, rather gaunt looking, thin man in his fifties, smartly dressed, wearing a dark pinstripe suit set off by a white shirt, black and grey striped cravat and wearing highly polished black shoes appears from a side waiting room.

'Good evening Sir, I am Mr James Clifton, funeral director and owner of this establishment. May I politely point out sir, that my receptionist, Mrs Ruth Cumberland, who has been with this company for the past twenty years always leaves these premises for home precisely at 4 30pm.'

With a slow wave of his arm he gestures towards reception.

'As you can see, my receptionist Ruth, has gone.'

Clifton theatrically looks at his wristwatch.

'It is now 4 57pm, this establishment closes at 5 pm. However, on rare occasions, I am delighted to offer my extended services for those who are late in paying their last respects to their deceased loved ones. However if one, like yourself sir, is here to arrange a funeral, well that takes time. If that was to be the case, could you please return tomorrow but I suggest earlier in the day when you will be made to feel more than welcome by my receptionist and dare I say, myself.'

'Hold on there fellow, I'm finding it hard to keep up. I'm not here to mourn neither am I here to arrange a funeral service. In fact I'm a close member of the Forrester family and if you could, as you so generously put it, extend your services to accommodate me at this late hour, I would be much obliged. I'm just making sure that matters regarding the funeral service are in capable hands and having just met you, boy, I am sure they are.'

'Yes sir they are thank you and you would be?'

'I'm Paul, a friend of the family. I take it Mr Dennis Forrester is laid out in the back for those wanting to pay their last respects?'

'If you mean is the late Mr Dennis Forrester at rest in the Chapel of Rest, then yes sir he is, but just as a temporary measure mind for Mr Forrester is soon to be in an open casket at the family home in Sandbanks, on a date closer to the funeral service.'

'Help me out here, do you keep a copy of all the visitors, I mean their names?'

'I can assure you sir that all who enter the Chapel of Rest, barring the dead of course, sign in, all names are printed and are accompanied by a signature.'

From under the desk Clifton produces a visitor's book. He thumbs through some of the last pages that bear an assortment of different handwriting styles, and stops. He hands it to Grant. Here, see for yourself.'

'Wow! I didn't realise Dennis was such a popular guy.'

'So it would seem sir.'

Grant spends a few seconds studying the list.

'Now Mr Clifton, knowing Mrs Forrester as I do, I can assure you she is a stickler for protocol and would very much like to send cards acknowledging all those who have paid their last respects to her late husband Dennis.'

Grant takes his mobile phone out from the inside pocket of his jacket and waves it under Clifton's nose.

'I have an idea, would you mind..?'

'Mind what sir?'

'If I take a photo of this list of names, I would have asked your secretary Ruth for a copy but, well...'

Grant points to the empty receptionist's chair then at his watch.

'Oh! I see, no not at all sir…. Oh! I see you already have.'

Grant gets the image up on the screen making sure it's legible.

'So, does your establishment oversee all the funeral arrangements?'

'Why, do you now foresee a problem, do you not approve?'

'Look, it's not like that, it's just that I'm under pressure. I've been nominated by the relatives not only to make sure all is going to go well but to arrange the wake, and as yet I have no times or date. What a headache. But it's all hush hush you must understand, no letting on to whoever might walk through your door it's a sort of surprise. Now, drawing upon your vast experience Mr Clifton, are you able to help me out here and give me a date for the funeral service?'

'No I am afraid not, but possibly in two to three weeks' time. It is not easy for all concerned you understand, especially me. There is an extraordinary amount of red tape, a lot of form filling and certain clearances are required.'

'I understand. Ok, but you must at least know how the service will run?'

'Ha, you must be referring to the 'Order of Service'. Let me explain... funeral services tend to be different, as is the cost, but generally speaking for a cremation the family would contact their chosen Funeral Director, which in this case c'est moi, whereby an appointment would be made to discuss the family's wishes, now that could be for a religious service or not. Not, is becoming the norm these days. Also there would be the financial matters to discuss for example the cost of the casket and the cost of cars, would it be a priest to preside over the service or would it be a celebrant, the choosing of hymns, music and flowers etc. Furthermore, in regard to Mr Forrester's funeral service, Mrs Forrester has made it quite clear she does not want a religious service so it will be up to me to decide which of my celebrants would be suitable to meet her requirements. In fact our most successful celebrant for non-religious services is Celebrant Peter North. I have others on my books, a whole list of them, but Peter is my favourite by far. It's no secret, only from the other celebrants you understand!' He sniggers. 'All funeral directors tend to have their favourite celebrant and they provided them with more work than the others, it's all hush hush you know. To be quite honest I feel our profession is becoming saturated with celebrants or so called celebrants. Where was I, ah, yes, back to Peter, well, he has got what you might say is a certain panache, he has a way with words and people, a special charisma one could also say.'

'So, you will be in contact with this Peter North soon.'

'Yes I will be. I'm sure the family will love him, they all do you know.'

'I mean, to tell him that he will be officiating at the service.'

'That's my intention, yes.'

'I will look forward to meeting him.'

'Oh, I regress sir, now, where was I, oh yes, I have not got around to explaining the Order of Service.'

'No forget it, it's ok. I'll drop by in a few days to find out if you have any up to date details, you know, place, date and time, all that stuff.'

'No sir, please with all due respect do not concern yourself with returning to this establishment for such information when I can just as easily let you know by phone. Write down your contact number and I will call you as soon as I know.'

'Why, thank you very much Mr Clifton that's very kind of you.'

No sooner had Grant written his contact number down than Clifton ushers him towards the exit.

'Now sir I'm about to close up shop, it's getting rather late, Bobby my partner, well, he does tend to worry if I'm late home.'

'OK my good man, but you won't forget to call now will you, I am relying on you.'

Grant mimics the voice of Arnold Schwarzenegger,

'*Or, I'll be back*! Sorry, always wanted to say that!'

'Really sir, now please, if you wouldn't mind it's getting late.'

As soon as Grant has left Clifton closes and locks the door and exchanges the 'Open' sign for 'Closed' and returns to reception to make a phone call.

'Hello Bobby love, sorry I'm late but I've had one of those days. Be a sweetie, will you, line up a gin and tonic for me. Be home soon, ciao.'

Grant makes his way back to the unmarked SUV. Guilford has her knees up with both bare feet resting on the dashboard. She shows her displeasure by ignoring him.

'Well Fay that was really useful.'

Silence from Guilford.

'I said that was really useful.'

'Really'

'Look I know you're pissed and I'm sorry okay.'

'Pissed, it goes well beyond being pissed believe me. Now get us out of here, drive on.'

'Aren't you interested what happened, you know, what I found out?'

'Write it up, DS Grant and put it on my desk by 9am tomorrow morning.'

'What the fuck Fay! Come on.'

'Drive.'

Grant turns the ignition on, before driving off he waits for the windows to partly de-mist.

'Fuck this, no.'

He turns the ignition off. 'You're getting good at that' she says sarcastically.

'Look, I managed to get a list of names and signatures of all of Forrester's visitors and James Clifton the manager was very helpful, in his fifties I would say and definitely gay, he said he would get back to me regarding all the funeral arrangements, times, dates and all that.'

Guilford goes to speak...

'And no, before you say it, I did not blow our cover, as far as he's concerned I'm just another family member and more than likely a nutter at that!'

'He got that right then.'

'So, we're good then?'

'For now, but do that again and I'll be looking for another partner and you'll be behind a desk pen pushing, you got that?'

'Yes.'

'Have you got that!'
'Yes for Christ sake, I've got it.'
'Good, then let's go.'

Chapter 7

Detective Chief Inspector Munro of the Fraud Squad addresses Officers of various ranks, in the briefing room of the recently built extension to the existing Head Office block.

'Thank you, your attention please,' the hum in the room quietens to silence. 'Due to one reason or another there have been a number of unsolved cases over these past few years. Case files have been kept on the back boiler and we seem to be accumulating quite a backlog. It has been agreed, by those above, and myself of course, that a new Fraud Cold Case Unit is to be set up and Detective Inspector Helen Smyth,' he points to where she is sitting. 'Has been tasked to oversee the new unit along with three officers to assist, who at great cost to the department may I say, have been seconded from other units.'

Everyone in the room looks about them, searching out the three new faces.

DI Smyth stands and faces all of her colleagues.

'Thank you Sir, if I may,' she addresses the three officers. 'Officers Oliver Baines, Saif Khair and Jane Devon you're with me,' the three officers stand. 'Now Sir if we can be excused?'

'Of course DI Smyth, carry on. But I would just like to say a few words before you and your team go.'

Under the gaze of fellow officers the three officers negotiate their way past those officers who are seated, to the front of the briefing room and line up alongside DI Smyth and Detective Chief Inspector Munro.

'On behalf of everyone here I would like to welcome the three of you into the fold and will, with the greatest of interest, follow your progress under the guidance of one of our DI's, DI Smyth, so thank you and good luck.'

There is a round of applause from everyone in the room. Smyth leads her team out. Detective Chief Inspector Munro's briefing resumes as the last of the officers pulls the door shut behind them.

The three officers follow DI Smyth through the corridors of the newly built extension into the dowdy corridors of the old office block. Eventually they come to a halt outside a sparsely furnished but large office. In an attempt to spruce it up new floorboard had been put down and a fresh coat of paint had been applied to the walls and ceiling. Placed about the room there are three modern cantilever desks, each with a computer and telephone and on each of these desks in a tray are cold case files. Three filing cabinets are placed against one of the walls and attached to one of the other freshly painted walls is a large whiteboard, on two stands are flipcharts with various coloured marker pens in each of their trays.

The officers, stand, gazing around the room. DI Smyth addresses them.

'Each of you have been chosen for your diligence, attention to detail, persistence and the ability to follow orders and most importantly get results. We are working to a time scale in which to deliver these results and in order for us to achieve that, this is how we are going to start. As you can see on each of the desks are case files. Each of you have been assigned some case files. They are grouped together by the dates the offences were recorded.'

DI Smyth points to one of the three modern cantilever desks.

'Officer Devon that will be your desk, you will find that your case files are the most recent.'

'Officer Khair,' she points to another desk. 'That will be yours. You will find that your case files are dated the oldest. And finally Officer Baines, you will find that your case files are dated in between Devon's and Khair's. My office is next door but can be reached through the adjoining door.'

'As you re-examine each of the cold case files I expect communication, I want to hear you talking to one another, shout across the room if necessary, get into a discussion, debate, air your thoughts, cross reference your findings, even your hunches. I want it to sound like the stock exchange in here. Use the white board, be creative, draw graphs. I like visuals. Air your comments and note your conclusions no matter how incredible or inconceivable they may seem, then, when all that is done, if we still have no answers, well, then we will bloody well swop desks and start again...... any questions?'

There is a pause as the three officers look towards one another.

'No....? Good, well let's do it, let's get to work.'

As if rehearsed, all three officers answer together.

'Yes Ma'am!'

*

Peter North parks outside the Milton's residence in Havant, Portsmouth. The address earlier emailed to him from Ruth, the receptionist at J.C. Funeral Services. He sits back taking in the design of the recently built five bedroom house and especially the range of high-end vehicles parked on its drive way.

He thinks, look at this place and man those cars, wow! They must be loaded, I can smell money.

North pulls the sun-visor down and looking into its mirror he checks that his teeth are still clean and gleaming then runs his finger through his hair and straightens his tie.

'Okay let's do it.' He says to himself.

He picks up the black leather zip-up briefcase from the passenger's seat. Exiting his car he makes his way along the driveway, stopping occasionally to admire some of the vehicles and at the same time checking-out his own reflection in some of the tinted windows. Nearing the front entrance North is fully aware that his approach is being picked up by the CCTV cameras moving, tracking his every move. He thinks, now that's something to bear in mind.

Through the stained glass windows of the porch North can't make out if the blurred image of the figure standing there is male or female, he only knows that it is someone and that they are waiting to greet him. He lightly taps on the front door, the distorted figure steps forward and the door is opened by a middle aged woman. North thinks, wow! She, is, a, looker alright.

38

'Good morning, you must be Peter? We've been expecting you. I'm Jean Milton, Margaret's daughter. Please come in and meet the family we are all in the conservatory.'

*

DI Fay Guilford and DS Paul Grant, from the SDCD9 Special Unit are requested to attend a meeting with their Detective Chief Inspector, Jane Edinburgh, who is based at the Human Exploitation Organised Crime Command in London.

'Ok bring me up to scratch, Fay.'

'Yes Ma'am, following the death of Mr Dennis Forrester we've stepped up our surveillance at the family residence in Sandbanks and lately we have had surveillance on J. C. Funeral Services, who is arranging the funeral service of Dennis Forrester, in the hope that gang members or other traffickers who are known to us, turn up to pay their last respects. It's possible they might be thinking it's less likely for them to be seen there than at the funeral service and if we get a bite it will be our chance to make an arrest and get that individual or individuals to work for us, because Ma'am, to be quite honest, our window of opportunity is running out and anyway we're due a break.'

'Look Fay, past experience tells us that it would take months even years to turn a trafficker, they will be scared of the repercussions, not only to them but to their families. Remember all the problems we had with Dennis Forrester. Yes, we could get one of ours to infiltrate the gang but that too is a long and bloody dangerous road. So we need to come up with something quick. I know you have already, but try contacting the dedicated brothels again to see if they can come up with anything new like new faces appearing on the scene or any news or recent tip offs about people who are about to be brought in, it's worth a try.'

'Yes Ma'am.'

'It has also been reported of late that a few more massage parlours and a strip club have opened, again, could well be worth a visit?'

'Yes Ma'am.'

'You mentioned the surveillance on Forrester's home address, how's that going?'

'Well Ma'am, over the last few months there has been a steady increase in their security, which is manned 24/ 7. There are checks on everyone entering the main and side entrances. Aerial reconnaissance shows that extra CCTV has been fitted around the perimeter and higher rear fences have also been erected.'

'Bloody hell, it sounds like Fort Knox.'

'Also Ma'am, there's a motorboat moored up alongside the jetty to the rear of the property. Intelligence confirmed by the Coast Guard.'

'Ma'am, looks like Forrester was expecting the worst and getting ready for plan B.'

'Better keep an eye on that one. OK you two, keep me up to speed. Close the door on your way out and my regards to all at Portsmouth.'

*

North enters the large lavish conservatory at the Milton's residence. Jean Milton introduces him to her mother Mrs Margaret Milton and to five others who are seated on a Cane Memphis sofa set.

'Mum, this is Peter he is going to talk on our behalf at dad's service.'

'Thank you for coming.'

'Thank you Margaret that's if I may call you Margaret.'

'That will be fine, won't it mum.'

'Yes Jean.' holding a handkerchief up to her eyes, Margaret sobs. 'Sorry, sorry.'

'Margaret may I offer my sincere condolences over the loss of your husband Andrew.'

'That's very kind of you. Please have a seat Peter.'

'Thank you Margaret.'

Having completed his visit, North stands outside the front door of the Milton's residence bidding farewell to Jean and Margaret, He makes his way along the driveway, gets into his car, places the black briefcase containing the information for the late Mr Andrew Milton's funeral service, on the passenger seat, opens the glove-box and reaches for his mobile phone, suddenly there is a tapping on the window, looking to his right he can see Jean Milton peering in at him. He thinks, for fuck sake's what's she want. He turns the ignition key to its first setting which allows him to lower the window.

'Jean! How can I help you?'

'I'm so glad I caught you before you left.'

'Why is there a problem?'

'No, no, far from it, just to say the time and date for your next visit, it was at a time when mum would be by herself.'

'That's right Jean.' He thinks, fuck they've had second thoughts and someone is going to be there with the old girl.

'I'm just letting you know that I will be able to make it after all. I have only just this minute called work to explain the situation and they said it would be fine for me to take the day off.'

North thinks, fuck, I'd better just let this one run its course.

'Well, thank you for letting me know Jean.'

'Thank you again Peter. You got far to go?'

'No, I'll make my way back to my office and start writing up the notes I took for the service. You do have a card of mine, I left it with your mother, just in case you come across some more information about your father that you would like me to add to the eulogy or even if you have a change of mind about how the Order of Service is to run.'

'Thank you.'

'Good. Jean don't hesitate calling. I'm just at the end of the phone'

She laughs, 'Better get back to mum.'

'Ok, see you.'

North watches as she makes her way pass the parked vehicles. He thinks what an ass and her breast wow! They swing like two wet boiled eggs in a hessian sack, beautiful.

Even more so, was she hitting on me? It could be another way in, possibly an inheritance.

Before driving off, North makes the call he was about to before Jean Milton made her appearance. He presses re-dial.

Chapter 8

82 year old Ida Summers sits alone in the front room of her 1950's style bungalow listening to her favourite radio station playing her favourite music from the1940's. She hums along to each of the melodies and as she does so she reminisces on her earlier life as a young woman.

She is startled out of her reverie when her landline rings. Before answering she slightly lowers the volume on the radio.

'Hello,' her voice sounds croaky so she clears her throat with a cough. 'Hello, you have reached the Summers.' residence, Mrs Summers speaking. Can I help you?'

'Ida, it's me, Peter, celebrant Peter North, you called me earlier, so sorry I missed your call. I've been very busy of late but I'm free to talk now if you are.'

'Peter…., one second, hold the line.' he hears the receiver being placed down as if on a hard surface and can hear Ida speaking to herself and shuffling about. A few seconds go past before she can be heard picking up the phone.

' Peter , I'm back, just turned the radio off, yes that's better, now, I am so glad you called me back, I thought you may have been too busy, and I was right in thinking that you had more important things to do than to speak to me.'

'Nonsense Ida, what could be more important than talking to you. Let's put it another way my work took priority, that's all.'

'You are a sweetie. 'Oh Peter, I do miss my Harry,' she starts to sniffle…'Oh dear…..anyway,' his mind is on Jean Milton. 'Peter it's so nice to hear your voice again, it does indeed put my mind at rest.'

He thinks, daft old cow.

'Now Peter we did agree that we would keep in contact with one another didn't we?'

'Of course we did, and Ida, I always keep my promises,' he thinks, only if there's something in it for me of course.

'Why Ida, I was just about to call you anyway and there you go beating me to it.'

'I do try to keep myself busy these days but everything feels so hollow and empty especially with not having my dear Harry around. Granted, some of my family do pop in occasionally but they only stay for a short while and I know they mean well and I should be grateful I realise they are all so busy with their own lives you see. Mind you, they never warn me you know, when they're coming, they just turn up, it's so inconvenient. Oh Peter I do miss my Harry so very much, it's not the same you know.' He hears her sniffle then blow her nose.

He mutters to himself God help me, but still, try and cheer the old bird up.

'Ida, have you heard about a group of very nice elderly people called The University of the Third Age often referred to as the u3a?'

'No I haven't. Oh dear should I have?'

'Yes, my work as a celebrant has put me in contact with a few women who are members and I think it's something you should consider. The u3a offer a variety of activities for their members, for example: Writing for Pleasure, Gardening, Wine Tasting, History and many others. Special guests are also invited along to their meetings to give talks on various subjects. If anything it would get you out and about and it would be a chance meet other people, mostly women, in your age group and make new friends while you're at it. There's bound to be a local one you can sign up to.'

'Well I'm not sure. I don't get out much now that my Harry has passed away. My confidence seems to have somewhat left me I'm afraid, and as for meeting new people well…'

'That's my point Ida, give it a go. You called me didn't you and that took confidence didn't it?'

'Yes I guess it did. No, you're right it does sound rather interesting. I just may take up your good advice.'

'Good for you. Now why don't I come round and pay you a visit so we can catch up whilst sharing a nice pot of your lovely tea?'

'Oh, that would be so nice. When do you think, sorry I'm being a bit too eager aren't I?'

'No you're not; it's a sign of confidence.'

'I can assure you that I will not be letting my family know, they are highly critical of just about everything I do these days and to be quite honest I am fed up with it. And to be quite truthful I can meet who I bloody well like to.'

'Ah! There's that confidence again, there's no stopping you now! I don't blame you as family can be very thoughtless at times, so well done you. Look whatever time or day suits you best really, oh, and I will supply the cakes!'

'That will do nicely Peter. As it's Friday today shall we say... next Wednesday?'

'Just checking my diary as we speak, let me see now, two family visits booked for the morning but free all afternoon. Perfect, say 1pm Wednesday afternoon?'

'A bit early for tea and cakes I think Peter but yes 1pm it is, my finest Bone China will at last see the light of day again, bye.'

Ida places the receiver down, turns the radio on, ups the volume and starts to joyfully hum along to the melodies being aired. Reaching across the dining table she slides the family album towards her and studies its well-thumbed pages.

*

Cold Case Fraud Unit Officers Baines and Khair are sat at their desks while Officer Devon stands in front of a large whiteboard writing various names and dates and cross referencing them with different coloured board pens.

'So far I keep getting amounts arranging from £3000 to £20,000 cropping up pretty regularly, how about you guys?'

'Well, to be quite honest Saif I've been working from a slightly different angle, building a profile of sorts. Whoever was, or still is, receiving these payments, and I'm only speculating here, felt safe in the knowledge that whatever took place was not going to be discovered for a long, long time, if at all. There is definitely an air of confidence, surrounding a sort of invulnerability about this character if you know what I mean, how about you Jane?'

'I agree, have you two noticed how many of these cases have been reported by a family member on behalf of another family member who had recently been widowed now deceased. I don't want to think the worst but it seems our suspect could very well be in the funeral game, crazy I know but we were told to think of every angle possible.'

'So we are in agreement then, singly each case leads nowhere but together a pattern is starting to emerge. We could be looking at a serial fraudster here. Let's keep at it.'

Devon who is studying the info on the whiteboard starts to fill in some of the blanks in a spider diagram. In the middle circle she writes 'Funeral' followed by a question mark, on the first legs she writes the values: £3000/£10,000 and £20,000 on the second leg: reported by family not victim.'

Chapter 9

Peter North is parked outside Ida Summers terraced house in Waterlooville, Portsmouth. He checks his mobile for missed calls, there is one but he doesn't want to hear it right now, doesn't want to be distracted from his next move so he switches to silent mode. Before getting out he looks into the rear view mirror and starts to slowly comb his hair. Today his hair is slicked back. He reaches over to the passenger's seat and picks up a box containing two chocolate eclairs that he had bought en route then makes his way to the front door and having rang the doorbell it doesn't take long for frail looking 82 year old Ida to answer.

'Ida, great to see you again, look, see, I've come bearing gifts!' He thinks, she's much older looking than I remember, but I'm not here to cosy-up.

'Oh goodie, do come in Peter, please come in. Make your way through to the back living room, you know where it is, and I will make us a nice pot of tea.'

He thinks, fuck it smells of old damp dogs in here.

As North makes his way to the back living room he looks around and listens out for anyone else who might be in the house. There is no-one except for a dog who is frantically scratching at the back door, trying to get in from the backyard. He thinks, I wouldn't put up with that shit.

Before making himself comfortable in one of the frayed armchairs he picks up the two heavily stained gold coloured scatter cushions. Holding one in each hand he hits them against each other, and then gives them a good shaking.

'That'll do I guess.' he mutters.

His attention is brought to the wall clock, it is 1pm, and he checks it against his wristwatch. He thinks, at least that's fucking working. It could be worth a bob or two at the auctions for whoever clears this house when she's dead and gone.

North's not waiting long before he can hear a rattling squeaky noise, and it's getting louder. He sits down in the armchair. Ida enters the living room pushing a tea trolley complete with cups, saucers, plates, teapot, milk, spoons, serviettes and two knives. She positions the tea trolley next to a coffee table and sits opposite North.

'Don't worry about that old dog of mine Betsy she'll soon settle in her kennel, just being nosey that's all. I swear one day she'll claw her way through that door. Now Peter, if I remember right you take milk but no sugar.'

'Spot on Ida, yes I do and I know that you enjoy a chocolate éclair filled with lovely fresh cream. Have I got that right?'

'Oh yes! Oh this is fun!'

North edges the box of cakes that he placed on the coffee table, towards her.

'Go on Ida, open the box, have a cake!'

She expresses great delight, 'Oh it's just like the TV gameshow me and my Harry loved to watch, now, what was it called oh yes 'Open the Box' and I do believe that it was hosted by a man called Hughie Green.'

He thinks, joy of joys, no idea what's she's on about, just open the fucking box will you woman.

'Oh Peter! It has been ages since I've been treated to a fresh cream chocolate éclair, absolute ages, but not both for me surely!'

'Absolutely not Ida, I should coco! One for you and one for me, you can't have all the fun you know!'

She pulls the tea trolley closer to her and using her arthritic hands she painfully picks up a cake slice and uses it to take the cakes out of the box then places each one on a small bone china plate. To her the delight is completed by adding a serviette.

'It can get a bit messy you know, time for tea Peter!'

'Yes, time for both, tea and cake.'

'I should say so.'

Having now chatted for well over an hour, the time on the clock now shows 2: 20pm.

North's had enough, he thinks. I can't waste any more of my fucking time here. She's either took the bait or she hasn't. Crunch time! He gambles and makes his move.

'Well Ida, I have had such a lovely time. And if I may say, you have been the perfect host. Time has just well, flown by, do you not agree?'

She looks back over her shoulder up at the walled clock.

'Is that the time already? Oh it's been such fun.' North stands up preparing to leave.

'So Ida, I must be on my way. Once again it has been a pleasure. You stay put and I will see myself out.'

He thinks, say something then, come on you old bat.

'Peter'

'Yes Ida.'

'Before you go,' He thinks about fucking time. 'I need to say what it is on my mind. Peter please sit down.'

He thinks 'Hook line and sinker, time to take!'

'Well, Ida my dear, this all sounds rather ominous.'

North sits down sliding the scatter cushions onto the floor.

'Are you okay Ida, is there something wrong?'

'No, no, no I'm fine, I really am, it's just that I have been slightly worried about you of late, in fact ever since your last visit, well, not so much as worried as concerned.'

'Really, what have you to be concerned about Ida?'

'Well dearie, now, I hope you don't mind me saying so.'

He thinks, for fucks sake get on with it woman.

'Not at all, tell me what's on your mind.'

'Earlier on, during your previous visit, that is, when we were planning my poor Henry's funeral service, you mentioned, what was the word now, diversify, yes that's the word; you were hoping to diversify into other areas of work. Only it sounded to me that you were having difficulty raising the finance required to make a success of things. £15,000 you said would be what was required.'

He thinks, should have upped that to £20,000.

'Yes Ida I did, but don't you go concerning yourself with that now will you.'

49

'But I am Peter, I am worried, worried for you and I want to help.'

He thinks, I need to test her. Will she keep her mouth shut?

'Ida you are a real love, but think of how your family would react to our little tea party and previous conversations let alone that you are prepared to help me out financially, well they would not be too pleased, not pleased at all.'

'Look dearie, what goes on within these four walls of mine is my concern and mine only. They, the family, may think my private affairs are theirs but they are not. So, I've been thinking, until your assets, which you mentioned are tied up for a year, what's the term you used 'frozen assets' yes frozen assets are accessible I am happy to cover the cost to tide you over. So, when I knew you were coming here today, I went to my bank and withdrew £15,000 from my savings just for you. You should have seen their faces, they looked absolutely stunned. The cashier called the bank manager over to talk to me. Bloody cheek, he tried to talk me out of it and wanted to know what it was going to be used for, but I was not having it. I told him that was for me to know and not him. After all, it's my money at the end of the day, not theirs.'

'You are one head-strong woman Ida and I greatly admire that. Look I make a point of not arguing with someone who has made their mind up and from where I'm standing Ida, well, you surely have made yours up, bless you.'

'Yes Peter I have, haven't I. You know what Peter I think I'm getting the hang of this confidence thing! More tea?'

*

'So Paul, which one of us is going to tell the DCI we've got jack shit to report regarding the trafficking gang's movements. Flip you, heads or tails,' Guilford flips a 10p coin in the air. 'Quick Paul it's your call!' She catches it then places it, covered, on the back of her hand. Go on then, call it, Heads or Tails?'

'What, oh yes err, Heads.'

'Tails, you lose.'

'Fuck that Fay! We'll go in together.'

50

'Paul if you ever go for promotion you'll need to grow a bigger pair of...'

Grant receives a call on his mobile. He recognises the caller's number to be that of James Clifton from J. C. Funeral Services. To get everybody's attention in the office in order for them to be quiet he frantically waves his hand in the air and uses a cut throat gesture by dragging his thumb across his throat. All goes quiet.

'Hello, Paul speaking.'

'Paul, this is James, Mr James Clifton, manager of J. C. Funeral Services. You asked me to contact you regarding the arrangements for Mr Dennis Forrester's funeral service.'

'Yes I did and thank you for getting back to me Mr Clifton.'

'Please call me James'

'Yes sure James.'

'The service will take place at the Portsmouth Crematorium in three weeks' time at precisely 2:30pm on the 15th of November and will be held in the Thoresby Chapel. Peter North, my most favoured celebrant, who I told you about, will be officiating. Mr Forrester's casket will be arriving at the family home two days prior to the service on the 13th of November. Now Paul, I hope that helps and it was a pleasure meeting you.'

'Thank you...'

'James.'

'James, yes, thank you and I really do appreciate your call.'

'No problem Paul, all part of the service, goodbye and a good morning to you. And if ever you are passing, well you know.'

'I will bear that in mind James. Thanks again, bye.

'Oh Paul, there is one thing though.'

'What's that?'

'The wake, I guess I will bump into you there at some point,'

'I'll keep an eye out for you. Like I said thanks for your help James. Bye.'

Grant places his mobile phone on his desk. Guilford and the team stare at him in anticipation. 'Yes!' He fist punches the air.

'Yes! Thanks guys.' The office returns to its busy hum of voices and telephone calls.

'Fay it's on! It's just been confirmed that the casket containing our Mr Dennis Forrester will be moved to the family home on Monday the 13th of November two days before the funeral on Wednesday 15th at 2:30 at Portsmouth Crematorium. Now apart from James I mean Mr Clifton having a crush on me, it's going to be our best opportunity to get eyes on a known trafficker and turn him or her to our way of thinking.'

'Well Paul, well done partner,' they give each other a high five.

'But between now and Forrester's home coming, we still need to step it up and look for another way and fast.'

Chapter 10

North parks in the grounds of Portsmouth Crematorium, mentally preparing himself for another funeral service as he rereads the service notes. The ring-tone, 'All Things Bright and Beautiful' sounds from his mobile phone. The name Zara Maxwell comes up on the screen. He thinks, well that didn't take you too long did it Mrs Zara Maxwell.

'Hello Peter North speaking.'

'Hi, this is Zara, Zara Maxwell.'

'Hi Zara, great to hear from you, how are you? Sorry that was a stupid question under the circumstances, forgive me.' He thinks; fuck what a stupid thing to say.

'That's ok. You know, I've have had so many family and friends say the same thing, can't blame them of course, you could say I've become immune!'

'Still I should have known better. Give me another go. Hi Zara it's great to hear from you again!' She laughs.

' Peter, I've been thinking about the conversation when we had at the crematorium, and you know what? You're right, we should meet up for that drink and talk about the good things in life, it may help me move on! Besides I've missed you.'

He thinks, that's my girl, this is the opening I knew was coming my way.

'Well, coincidently, and it is coincidently by the way, I will be in your area tomorrow, I could be at yours for say, three o'clock?'

'He thinks, idiot you're sounding desperate, ease up.

'Of course Zara if that's inconvenient, being at such short notice, we can always rearrange.'

'No, tomorrow will be great, can't be soon enough for me actually. Must warn you though, we will be alone in this big house of mine, oh, except for one of my housemaids,'

'Zara I'm big and ugly enough to take care of myself.'

'Still, it doesn't pay to be too defensive though! You know, holding back. Oh, and pull straight up onto the driveway will you. I'll be waiting. Bye for now.'

North pushes himself back into his seat by straightening out his arms, pushing against the steering wheel. He speaks out loud 'As if I would hold back. Money and sex a great combination, what was it the big guy used to say on TV, I love it when a plan comes together! Wow, she's definitely up for it.' He looks at his reflection in the rear-view mirror. 'Come on you, pull yourself together you've got a funeral service to do.'

He combs his hair, reaches for his briefcase and places the service notes he has been going over inside. Having exited his car he walks across the grounds of the crematorium towards the chapel where in thirty minutes time he will be officiating at the funeral service of Mr and Mrs Samuel Hawkins.

North had been given prior warning by Ruth, the receptionist from J.C. Funeral Services, before visiting the family that Mr and Mrs Hawkins had been killed in a hit and run road accident, the culprit or culprits, as of yet, had not been caught. On discovering what had happened to the Hawkins, North was taken back to the time when he took part in the coalition invasion of Iraq when the base camp from which he and his team were operating was partly devastated by a suicide bomber. His truck loaded with explosives smashed its way through the main barriers, striking and killing three of the guards before continuing, under armed fire, to drive deeper into the camp before exploding.

During his visit to the Hawkins family, North found himself having to sit through and suffer as each family member vented their anger and frustration towards him over the fact that justice had not yet been done. His attempt at collating information about the lives of Mr and Mrs Hawkins for the eulogy became a near impossibility, but from the scraps of information he managed to get, not for the first time, he had patched something together.

Outside the chapel mourners from the previous service were hugging, shaking hands and bidding each other farewell.

On entering the chapel North sees that the vicar is still in the process of collecting his service notes from the lectern. He thinks; hurry up old man I've got to get my shit sorted. North walks to the lectern.

'Good morning vicar.' He thinks, you're the miserable one right, you pompous fucking old git.

The vicar looks down his nose at him. 'Oh, yes, errm good morning.' He finishes collecting his notes and scurries off. North has learned to expect such a reaction from certain members of the cloth, the ones who try to make him and no doubt other celebrants feel unauthentic unworthy of being able to parallel what they the clergy can offer the bereaved. But then he thinks, fuck it, FUCK HIM.

Chapter 11

As North approaches Zara Maxwell's beachfront house it's raining heavily and the coastal winds are blowing hard. The electric gates to the property are open giving access to the driveway. Having swung into the parking area he cuts the engine, collects his thoughts and makes a mad dash through the pouring rain to the front door. He is no sooner there than the door is opened by Zara Maxwell.

'Oh! Come straight in Peter! Quickly, you're getting absolutely drenched!'

She stands to one side as North hurries past her. He thinks, wow she smells divine.

'Man that rain is heavy and really cold.' He looks down at himself. 'Look at me I'm wet through!' They both laugh.

'Quick Peter hand me your jacket.' He smells alcohol on her breath. 'In fact, remove both your jacket and your shoes.' As he crouches down to unlace and take off his wet shoes he notices how smooth and tanned her long legs are and when he stands up she sees his athletic frame as his damp white shirt clings to the contours of his body.

'Well Zara, not the entrance I intended to make.'

'You're here and that's all that matters. Go through to the kitchen lovely' she points across the large reception area to a hallway, 'Just along there, I'll hang your jacket up to dry out a bit. And don't hesitate in making yourself at home, I will be with you in a jiffy, oh and another thing, you'll find there are plenty of paper kitchen towels there to help dry off with.'

With his hair and jeans still dripping wet, North tries to avoid leaving a trail of water stains on the light oak flooring as he makes his way to the kitchen. He looks for the paper towels and finds them hanging under one of the units and tears a handful off. Having rubbed them over his hair he then looks at his reflection in the glass door of the microwave, he styles it as best he can with a comb which he takes from his back pocket.

He grabs some more kitchen towels and pats down the front of his jeans. Unable to figure out which low level unit was hiding the bin he places the wet paper towels to one side of the kitchen worktop.

Pulling out one of the stools from under the island unit he sits admiring the décor and is particularly struck by the Moroccan style wall tiles above the sink and the way they highlight the geometric kitchen print set and how the white floating shelving enhances the calming earthy colours of the other walls and units. He thinks, wow, this is class man.

Zara Maxwell enters, wearing a low cut blouse and a tighter shorter skirt, a much shorter skirt than she had on when he arrived. He thinks, 'Any shorter she may as well just be wearing nothing.'

'That's better Peter, you look more human now.'

He thinks, wow I'm also feeling right pumped up, better play it cool though.

'Well Zara, like I said, it wasn't exactly the entrance I wanted to make!' But….'

'And like I said Peter, you're here and that's all that counts. So, let's have a drink!'

As she stands on tip toe and stretches to one of the many high level fridges for a bottle of champagne, her skirt rises showing her legs to where they meet the cheeks of her bottom. Reaching to a low level unit for two glasses, her low cut blouse displays the full extent of her cleavage. Placing the glasses on the granite work surface, she uncorks the bottle and slowly pours the champagne into two glasses then sits on a stool with her long tanned legs crossed, on full display of course. He thinks, fuck, now I really am pumped, perks of the job!

'Well Peter! All that rain, I find it quite mystic really, sort of sensual in a way, don't you think! I connect to people like that they can sense it from me. Cheers, here's to us.'

'To us Zara, cheers!' They clink glasses before taking a sip.'

'You really do have a nice place here Zara it looks even more luxurious than I remember.'

'Now, when you were last here, discussing my late husband's funeral service, I felt a strong connection with you and I know you did with me. It all became clearer during our walk and talk in the gardens of the crematorium, you do remember our little chat don't you?'

'Of course I do.'

'Good, it was almost as though you were flirting with me and don't deny it.'

'Well I…'

'I knew you were! You naughty man you.'

'Zara, I was about to say like-wise.'

She places a well-manicured hand on his knee.

'You must like your job, you do it so well. There is an art to putting people at ease, taking the worry out of the reality of it all, you know, the death, the loneliness of it all.'

'Well Zara, I pride myself on it, it does my reputation no harm.'

'Reputation, now you've got me worried! what sort of reputation I wonder!'

'But you know what! My future lies elsewhere; I have bigger fish to fry.'

She edges her stool even closer him.

'Elsewhere you say, so tell me then, I'm intrigued, tell me about this future of yours.'

He thinks, bull-shit time, money making time. 'Well if you're really that interested,' he thinks I know what she's interested in. 'I'm in the process of buying a pub that's up for sale located in Cumbria, a beautiful part of the country. Have you ever been?'

'I've heard of it but never been.'

'You should.' Then he thinks that isn't your style though is it Zara. You'd rather climb the escalators in Harrods than climb the Cat Bells.

'You know what Peter, I can see you as a publican, I really can. Bet you do well, especially with all the ladies, it won't be just the beer you'll be pulling! So go on then, tell me when is all this going to take place?'

'Well it should have happened last year but as my assets, amounting to £30,000, are frozen and won't be available for another eighteen months I've been unable to move on with the deal and there's every chance I might miss out.'

'By the way.'

'What's that?'

'Were you?'

'Was I what?'

'Were you hitting on me?' He thinks, fuck she wasn't listening was she, not interested one bit, got to get her back onto the subject of money.'

'Zara it's criminal how banks are allowed to keep hold of someone's money when at the end of the day it's not theirs.'

'I agree totally. Well, was you hitting on me?' He thinks, for fuck sake.'

'And if I were to say yes?'

'Well if you were to say yes. 'She stands up, takes hold of his hands and eases him up to a standing positon. 'Well, if you were to say yes I would be so grateful and would be into it big time, does that shock you?'

'Shocked? No. interested? Very.'

North places his hands on her hips and pulls her closer. He thinks, the money matter can wait. There's far better ways of getting what I want.

'And the best way to capture all your interest Mr Celebrant would be to?'

North reaches out behind her and picks up the two glasses and the bottle of champagne.

'Well, the best way would be for us to go somewhere a bit more comfortable and a bit more private.'

'I can organise that, just follow me.'

She leads him up the bespoke oak staircase to one of the five lavish bedrooms.

'Make yourself comfy while I pop to the bathroom.'

North stands admiring the bedroom, its high ceilings, bespoke fitted wardrobes and oversized bed ticks all of his boxes for how, in his opinion, a bedroom should be. He places the glasses and bottle of champagne on one of the bedside tables and having been in other women's bedrooms many times before, he confidently and casually removes his Armani watch and places it on the same bedside table, then unbuttons and takes off his now nearly dry Eton White shirt and hangs it over the back of one of the chairs. so it doesn't crease.

He stands admiring himself as he poses in front of one of the many mirrors, flexing the muscles in the front and back of his torso and arms, checking that his new diet, formulated to make him looked ripped, is working. Satisfied, he unceremoniously hops from one foot to another as he tries to take off the damp socks that cling to each foot.

Leaving his Armani jeans on North crawls up across the bed and sits against the headboard. Continuing to admire the bedroom's décor, he waits.

Maxwell walks from the en suite, across the bedroom and sits at a dressing table, wearing no more than matching bra and pants. North thinks, wow! What a body, she's fucking sex in motion. In the mirror of the dressing table, she sees North's reflection, his athleticism and good looks looking back at her and smiles at him. Slowly removing her earrings, she places them in a velvet-lined box and from one of the drawers she produces a miniature remote control.

As she walks across the bedroom towards North the shutters silently and slowly unwind from the top of the three large bedroom windows that overlook the well maintained gardens and close. A soft reddish glow emanates from wall mounted lights.

Reaching the bed, she crawls upon it on her hands and knees to where North sits, legs stretched out. She sits astride him, unbuckles his leather belt and undoes the first three buttons of his Armani Jeans revealing the top of his black briefs with the name Hugo Boss printed in the waist band. North pulls her towards him. She pushes him back against the headboard.

'No, let me, lay back.'

Zara slides down the bed on all fours so that her face is in line with North's navel and ripped abdominal muscles. She gently licks and bites her way up to his chest. North undoes her bra revealing her large heavy breasts that now rest against his six-pack. He pulls her up to eyelevel. By lifting his backside up then his knees he slips his briefs and jeans down to his ankles, kicking them off. He rolls Zara on to her back, the hardness of him pressing against her pants, she gasps. Now he's in control. He leans forward gently kissing her neck then each of her hard erect nipples. She gasps even louder as he caresses both breasts with his strong hands kissing and sucking them harder. North moves down on her, he runs his tongue teasingly along her inner thighs coming to rest at the edge of her wet pants. Zara heaves with pleasure. His tongue slips in under her pants, searching, penetrating. She grabs hold of North's hair with both hands. His hand reaches up cupping both her breasts before sliding both hands under each of her buttocks he lifts pulling her harder to his mouth. She grips the bars of the headboard and starts thrusting her hips in circular motions, groaning with sheer pleasure. North wants her to keep excited, begging for it, not to cum right yet so he kneels up, closes her legs together and pulls the soaked pants off along her long tanned legs. She looks down and sees his penis is hard and wanting. Zara parts her legs and lifts her hips up as North edges forward.

*

DI Smyth has arranged a team meeting at the Cold Case Fraud Unit office.

'Ok everyone; let's see how far we have come. You have all worked diligently since being here and produced some good leads. I had a meeting with the Boss earlier and briefed him on our latest findings. I requested that we are notified if any new cases displaying the same Intel as ours come in. We have arrived at the point where we will be doing some good old fashioned police leg work. We will be re-visiting and talking to the victims in order to get a clearer picture, narrow things down. So, we are starting with the cases which are somehow connected in one way or another. By now you all have a good idea which cases they are. Doing this may help us to clarify events, help us to re-evaluate each case or even turn up some fresh information and leads.'

Lying naked, Zara rest her head across North's bare chest.

'Christ! I needed that. I've been under so much pressure of late. It's amazing what a fuck can do, oooh yes, what a fantastic release. More please more!'

'Hey, slow down gorgeous, there's plenty more where that came from, I promise, but more of that expensive champagne first.'

They both sit up resting back against the headboard and finish the drink that's left in their glasses.

'Another bottle I think.'

'Best not Zara, I'm driving.'

'Oh, don't be a party pooper! Come on, more champagne to celebrate the beginning of our fantastic relationship, and.... our new business venture together of course!'

'Business venture! What business venture?'

She sits astride him. 'Yep, first I'm going to write you out a cheque for £30,000 right now!' She stretches across, carefully so as not to come off him, to one of the bedside cabinets, slides open a drawer and pulls out a cheque book and pen. Placing the open cheque book on North's chest she writes a cheque for the amount of £30,000. Sitting upright she places the cheque in her cleavage, North leans forward slowly and removes the cheque with his lips, he then falls back on to the crumpled silk sheet, takes the cheque in hand and reads it aloud. '£30,000 God you're wonderful.' He thinks, boy, oh boy, I fucking love this way of getting money, the gullible slut.

'We're going into partnership Peter! But it must be our little secret of course. I will be one of those, what you call a silent partner, don't want tongues wagging now do we. Talking of tongues I could really do with some more of your loving, I think I deserve it, don't you?'

'Before we do, how about that other glass of champagne'

'All in good time big boy, no rush,' She leans forward. Her heavy breasts hover above his chest, her nipples hardening as every now and then they touch his skin. 'Zara, I'm not going anywhere right yet!'

Chapter 12

One week later.

In the lounge of 'The Swan' North is relaxing as he reads through the Obituaries column printed in one of the local Portsmouth newspapers. He has learnt from experience that by doing this there is a good chance of discovering a snippet or two of extra information he could add to the eulogy he is formulating for the upcoming funeral service for Mrs May Derringer. During the home visit the husband had very little to say about his deceased wife, which was not that unusual to come across. It was possible that a family member or friend may have put something more about her life in the Obituary column that he could use.

Mia is busy at the bar, which is somewhat noisier and busier than usual, especially for an afternoon shift.

*

Zara Maxwell paces around her living room, drink in hand. She puts a cigarette in her mouth, picks up a solid silver cigarette lighter and after many failed attempts to light it she screams and throws it against an original Kerry Darlington painting 'Elysian'. The lighter falls to the floor leaving a corner of the picture frame cracked. Annoyed with herself she screams even louder then re-dials North's number.

*

North's mobile plays its ring-tone, *'All Things Bright and Beautiful'*.

To enable him to hear over the noisy small group of office workers who are celebrating a retirement, he walks into the snug, where it's quieter, mouthing to Mia that he won't be long, he takes the call.

On recognising the caller to be Zara Maxwell, he hesitates. He thinks, fuck I can do without this right now.

He answers 'Hi Zara great to hear from you, been meaning to get in touch but been a bit busy I'm afraid. So how are you?'

'How am I, you've got a bloody nerve asking me how I am! I'll tell you how I am, apart from not hearing from you, I feel fucking used and taken advantage of.'

'Zara, come on now, it's only been, what, a week, not even that, I mean what's the problem?' North thinks, this bitch has been drinking and having second thoughts about the money. I knew it was a possibility but this soon no way. I knew this one would be trouble.

'The problem is it was wrong, it was wrong doing what I did, what we did.'

He thinks, yep here comes the fucking guilt trip and this one can't handle it, better take this outside.

'Hold the line Zara, I won't be a second.'

North places the call on hold as he walks out of the snug and makes his way outside to the car park. He gets into his car and resumes the call. 'Ok, sorry about that Zara, you were saying?'

'For fuck sake, are you sure you have the time to take my call, you know, to talk to me, I mean I wouldn't want to be fucking interrupting anything important.'

'Look, why are you like this, why are you doing this. You're pissed aren't you?'

Yes I'm pissed and I'm pissed off with you. I want it back, the cheque that is, I want it back.'

'Fuck, sorry love, major problem. I've banked it.'

'Well withdraw it. Get it out and drop it off back here. I'm not going to be made a fool of. I do know people you know, the sort you wouldn't want to mess about with.'

'Zara, don't you think you're overreacting, I mean for Christ sake it's only been a short while since we…'

'You're not listening North, I want my money back or else.'

'Well shit Zara if ever there was a threat made that was it, I'm sorry you feel that way. I mean you invite me around to yours then come on to me big time. What man in their right mind would turn that down, so give me a fucking break will you and just piss off.'

'Why, you bastard! Look, for the last time, I want my money back you big fuck, all of it mind and I want it back now!' She screams down the phone. 'Are you fucking listening to me?'

'Zara, now you're really are pissing me off. Try and see it this way, it was the price you paid for a good seeing to. Don't get me wrong, I did enjoy it. '

'Fuck you, fuck you North. I'm going straight to the pol...'

'I wouldn't if I were you, you crazy bitch!'

'And why's that, who's to stop me, you?'

'Think about it, you will be jeopardising everything. Are you really going to risk your family disowning you 'cos that's what will happen when they find out you've been shagging the man who buried your old man, and that you paid £30,000 for the pleasure? Not just your family, how about your friends, because it would all come out in court, that's where this would all end up. Do you really think they would want to know you after that? Of course the newspapers would love it, readers love a scandal. All sounds a bit desperate doesn't it Zara. So do us both a favour, and fuck off.'

He cancels the call. Maxwell shouts down the phone. 'North, North can you hear me? Are you still there, you fucking bastard?'

Angrily she pours herself another glass of wine, the one that empties the bottle. She sits, cursing as she randomly flicks through a small case of business cards that belonged to her late husband Donald. Under M she comes upon a business card, Mayfair, John, Private Detective.

Chapter 13

Inside an office in a rundown office block in Portsmouth a phone rings, Private Detective John Mayfair, Afro-Caribbean, six foot three with a heavy build, answers the call.

'Mayfair speaking, how can I help?'

'Mr Mayfair, you won't know me, but my name is Zara Maxwell. Some time ago you were hired by my husband, I mean my now late husband Donald Maxwell.'

'I've worked for a lot of people down the line Mrs Maxwell. Trouble is my ability to retain people's names is not my best forte. Now if I were to check my files against your husband's name, you say? Donald Maxwell.'

'Yes'

'Well, I'm guessing you'd be right or we wouldn't be having this conversation now. So Mrs Maxwell how can I help you?'

'Ok, I remember overhearing Donald telling someone that you have a reputation for getting the job done and anything that needs returning gets returned.'

'I like to work on that premise sure, it does my reputation no harm, but occasionally some things just don't work out, but I do have my ways sure I do. You could say I work somewhere between the gutter and the law. So, again Mrs Maxwell how can I help you?'

'Mr Mayfair, I need you to help me,' She starts to cry. 'I'm going fucking crazy here.'

'Look Zara, can I call you Zara?'

'Sure.' She continues crying.

'Zara, you're obviously very upset; this conversation would be better arranged for another time.'

'No! I need something doing right now, ASAP, not fucking later or whenever.'

'Ok, ok, face to face, your place tomorrow, not my office as it's err, well.'

Mayfair looks despairingly around at the wallpaper and paint that's peeling off the damp walls of his office.

'My office is in the middle of... yeah of ...being renovated. Say 10am?'

'Yes, let me give you my address, like you say, files aren't always that reliable are they.'

'I guess you got me there Zara! Fire away.' Mayfair tucks the mobile under his chin as he writes the address on the edge of a newspaper which he tears off and puts in the empty in-tray.

'OK got it, Oh, and Mrs Maxwell, if after you've slept on it you've had a change of mind, give me a bell, early mind, I'm a very busy man, there's people out there who need my help.'

'Believe me Mr Mayfair as far as I'm concerned you're hired. Having slept on it you say, well I don't sleep nowadays.'

'Well, you're in good hands now so try to calm down and relax. Goodbye Mrs Maxwell.'

Mayfair leans back into his one and only prize possession, a posture executive leather office chair. With his legs out stretched he rests his feet on top of a small filing cabinet. Mr Sherlock Holmes, a black cat with sharp blue eyes, jumps up onto his lap, purring.

'Well, Mr Sherlock Holmes looks like one of those rich white folk living in the Sandbanks area is in need of our detective skills. Could be just what we've been waiting for to get us out of this run down shit hole of an office. What do you think Mr Holmes?'

Mr Holmes purrs.

*

A call is patched through to DI Smyth from the main Fraud Squad Office.

'DI Smyth.'

'Helen, Chief Inspector Munro, I've been handed a file that may relate to some cases you are looking into. I will be sending it across for you to look at. Keep me up to scratch.'

'Thank you Sir, will do.'

Smyth calls her team to her office.

'It looks like we may have an important piece of the jigsaw coming our way, the boss is sending across an up to date case file that we might be very interested in.'

An officer knocks on the partly opened door, walks in and places the file on the nearest desk.

'With the compliments of DCI Munro.'

He turns and leaves. DI Smyth opens the file and begins to read. officers Baines, Devon and Khair try to get clues from Smyth's facial expression as to what it is she is reading. She continues to reads, turning turn the pages.

'Ok, listen in guys. We have a Mr James Summers who claims that his late mother Ida Summers handed over the sum of £15,000 to whom they don't know. Apparently it was discovered when the son James Summers was going through his late mother's finances. An amount of £15,000 was also discovered as an entry she had put in her diary, no names I'm afraid, just that she withdrew £15,000 from her bank. Mr Summers is convinced that whatever went off was a scam. Now what stands out here guys, apart from anything else, is the locality and the £15,000 tag and bearing in mind it is once again a family member of a deceased loved one, who contacted Fraud. This all sits well with the MO of some other cases. Devon, coat on, you're with me, Baines and Khair I want you to speak to the original interviewing officers and get copies of their interview. Meanwhile Devon and I will be paying Mr James Summers a visit.'

Chapter 14

Private Detective John Mayfair comes to a halt at the closed electric gates of Zara Maxwell's property in Sandbanks. He pulls alongside the free-standing intercom. He edges the car forward until the long bonnet of his red 1960 left-hand drive Ford Galaxy is millimetres from touching the electric gates. He shuffles across to the passenger's seat and reaching out of the window he presses the call button. A low whirring sound comes from the CCTV as it moves, bringing him into focus to the viewer. A male voice comes from the intercoms speaker.

'Can I help you?'

'John Mayfair, I've an appointment with Mrs Maxwell.'

He shows his ID card by holding it up angled towards the lens of the CCTV camera.

There is a pause before a buzzer sounds as the lock on the front gates disengage and start to slowly open. Before the gates are fully open Mayfair's back in the driver's seat, hits the accelerator and powers through the gap. He slows down as he makes his way along the herringbone patterned brick surface. But he can't help thinking: rich white folk entrance only, deliveries and black people use rear entrance, yes sum boss. Such thoughts have followed Mayfair around all his life.

Zara Maxwell waits in the gravel-stoned parking area to greet him. Mayfair comes into sight, the tyres of the Galaxy crunch against the gravel-stone surface. Pulling up alongside a silver Mercedes-Benz, A-Class, he exits the Galaxy and walks towards her, thinking, wow what a babe, is that her.

'Mrs Maxwell?.... John Mayfair.'

'Oh, I wasn't expect..., oh nothing. Thank you for coming Mr Mayfair. Please, follow me.' Mayfair thinks, you weren't expecting a black guy now were you Mrs Maxwell.

As they walk towards the main entrance of the house. Mayfair takes this opportunity to cast his eyes over the stunning sea view.

'Wow! Nice place you got here Mrs Maxwell.'

'It'll do.'

'Guess you don't get too many black folk living in an area like this, you know, being Sandbanks and all.'

'That's one hell of a presumption you just made there Mr Mayfair, you do yourself and others of your persuasion a disservice. In actual fact you'll find there are many, as you say, black folk, living in Sandbanks who are very good friends of mine.'

Once inside the designer-built house Mayfair is led into the high-spec kitchen. Maxwell pulls a stool out from under one of the island units and sits, Mayfair follows suit. She reaches for a bottle of vodka and uncaps it.

'Drink, Mr Mayfair?'

'Not for me thanks, too early, but go ahead.' She does.

'Now, you wouldn't be judging me would you Mr Mayfair?'

He thinks, what, like she wouldn't be judging me because I'm black. He ignores the question.

'So Mrs Maxwell, how can I help you? And by the way drop the Mr, just call me Mayfair.'

She places her now empty glass on the work surface.

'Look....what I'm about to tell you, well, it's rather a sensitive matter, something that must remain strictly between us and only us.'

He thinks, If I had a pound for every time someone said that I could be living here.

'Don't you worry Mrs Maxwell, whatever it is it isn't going any further than these four walls. So again, how can I help?'

'Look, this isn't easy for me you know to tell you.'

He thinks that's what they all say, but they always do in the end. She refills her glass with more vodka.

'Take your time Mrs Maxwell I'm all ears,' but I haven't got all day.'

She takes a deep breath.

'Okay, I gave, or rather lent, £30,000 to someone I thought I could trust. It was a mistake.' Mayfair thinks, it always is, I make a living out of people making mistakes and their regrets.

'I've asked for it back but to be quite blunt I was told, in no uncertain terms, to fuck off.'

'When did you hand over the money Mrs Maxwell and if you don't mind me asking why £30,000, that's a lot of money.'

'I handed it over a week ago, it was a cheque not cash. I've since found out it's been cashed. Why? Well, he had a business venture in mind and I wanted to be a part of it.'

'So, have you've seen this guy, I'm assuming it is a guy, since handing over the cheque?'

'You're right it is. No, I tried calling him many times, and finally, eventually I managed to get through to him.'

'And how did that go?'

'I considered myself to be quite reasonable with him at first, but he wouldn't have it, no, the fucker wouldn't have it.' She downs her drink.

He thinks, another drink, I need her to be thinking straight not pissed.

'And this person, I guess it's someone you know?'

'Oh my God no, here comes the part I've been dreading.'

She goes to pour another drink; Mayfair puts his hand over the top of the glass. She glares at him.

'Mrs Maxwell, I rather you didn't, I need you to be thinking clearly. I need the facts.' She pushes the bottle of vodka to one side.

'He's a Celebrant. The first time I met him was when he came here to arrange my husband's funeral service.'

'A puzzled look crosses Mayfair's face, he holds up both hands.

'Woo, stop there Mrs Maxwell, he's a what?'

'You know, a fucking Celebrant, one of those people who speak at funerals, an officiator, an orator, oh I don't know. What the fuck Mayfair, does it really matter what the fucking hell he is or what the fuck he isn't. I fancied him, the celebrant that is, when he came round here to discuss my husband's funeral service with me, I know, God knows it's shameful of me, I shouldn't have but I did.' She grabs hold of the bottle of vodka, thinks twice before placing it back down.

'I've heard a lot worse. Three things Mrs Maxwell, first of all, I'm sorry to hear about your husband. Secondly, did you screw this guy and thirdly, leave that cap on real tight now or I'm out of here.'

'Okay, Okay, no I bloody well didn't screw him...Christ what am I saying yes I fucking did. Look Mayfair does it make a difference. I'm going to be straight with you, we had a sort of something going and yes we got it together all right. I lent him money and that's that, now I want it back. God, if my family ever found out about this, he was right you know when he said they would disown me. I've been a complete fucked up idiot.'

'So this guy warned you that it was in your own interest to keep quiet?'

'Well he is right isn't he, If I told the police or confided in a member of the family, it wouldn't be long before it's out there would it, it would go around like wild fire. And apart from losing my family I would be totally humiliated and ashamed, unable to show my face in public. Some already think I'm a gold digger marrying a man three times my age. They would love this if they got to hear about it. I need to keep a fucking lid on this.'

'So, you decided to call me. You did the right thing Mrs Maxwell. I guess you're not the first to be scammed by this guy. I mean, him getting close, taking advantage of a widow's vulnerability, the lonely grieving women syndrome.'

'Well thanks a lot mate!' Her sarcasm builds up to a crescendo. 'That fucking well sure makes me feel a whole lot fucking better!' She unscrews the cap off of the bottle of vodka and pours out a glassful and takes a large gulp.

'Look Mrs Maxwell, I'm going to need a name and anything else you have for me to go on. I can always come back when you're calm and thinking straight.'

'No, no please I'm fine, I'm fine. No more drink, I promise,' she screws the cap back on the bottle. 'His name is Peter North. He was introduced to me through J. C. Funeral Services who are based on the High Street in Portsmouth...Well go on.'

'Well go on what?'

'Aren't you going to write this down?'

'No need. Can you give me a description of this guy? And I'm going to need you to forward his contact number'

'He's good looking, very fit and has a Hugh Jackman, the actor that is, look about him.'

'And?'

'And what, that's it.'

'Nooooo worries Mrs Maxwell, I'll google an image. Hugh Jackman you say, but this North guy works for J.C. Funeral Services right.'

'That's right.'

'Ok, so we know that much about him at least. I've worked with less. Now I don't come cheap Mrs Maxwell, there's plenty of cheap out there, cheap in my books equates to disappointed customers, with me you get what you pay for which is always a satisfactory outcome, so in hiring me you've hired the best. Okay that raps it up for the time being, I'll be in touch.'

'What, you're leaving!'

'I reckon so, I've got all I need for the time being.'

'Well, if you're sure.'

'I'm sure, I'll see myself out. Oh, and if you do hear from this guy, say nothing about our little meeting, but I'll be interested in what he says and if he happens to have a change of mind and wants to settle up with you, you let me know asap, I will bill you up until that time.'

Mayfair stands up, walks out of the kitchen, crosses the large entrance hall and before reaching the front door he hears Maxwell call out to him.

'You just do what the fuck needs to be fucking done Mayfair! Do you hear me!'

'I hear you Mrs Maxwell, I hear you.' He closes the door behind him and walks across the driveway to where his car is parked.

Now, alone in the kitchen, Zara Maxwell begins to sob heavily 'Whatever needs to be fucking done.' She uncaps the bottle of vodka and pours another drink.

Chapter 15

DI Smyth and Officer Devon arrive at a house in the Clanfield area of Portsmouth, where James Summers, son of the late Ida Summers resides.

A woman opens the front door to them.

'Mrs Summers?'

'Yes.'

'I'm Detective Inspector Smyth of the Cold Case Fraud Squad,' She shows her ID card. 'And this is Officer Devon. May we come in where it would be more private to talk?'

'Oh yes, of course, please do come in.'

She leads Smyth and Devon to the front room and invites them to sit down. As they do so Mr Summers enters the room. They both stand.

'Oh! Hello, who is this love?'

'James, this is Detective Inspector Smyth and her colleague Officer Heaven, so sorry, I mean, Devon, Officer Devon from Fraud.'

'Oh, I wasn't expecting you today. Have there been any developments? Only, I spoke to your lot, well it must be, what, two weeks ago now. Please take a seat.'

'Mr Summers, we, at the Cold Case Fraud Unit work alongside our colleagues from the Fraud Squad and look into unsolved past cases and it seems there may be some similarities to a case we are looking in to. You gave my colleagues a full statement, but my officer and I would like to hear it from you, in your own words if you don't mind.'

'Well, I can't remember word for word, the exact words that are in my statement that is but…basically, my dear mother Ida passed away recently, a very sad time as we had only lost my father a few months earlier. Whilst sorting out my mother's funeral service and her personal and financial affairs, it came to light that mother had withdrawn a large amount of cash from her building society in the sum of £15,000. Of course we knew nothing about this it came as a complete shock I tell you, a bloody big shock.'

'And you have no idea at all why your mother would have made such a large withdrawal of money?'

'As I told your colleagues, no, not a clue, at her age she really didn't want for much, well you don't do you when you're that old.'

'Do you think Ida may have had debts to pay off that you maybe didn't know about?'

'No, definitely not, we would have known. Pattie my wife and I called in on mother regularly to make sure she was keeping well and that the bills were being paid as there are no other family members who could have you see.'

'Would she have let strangers into her house?'

'Definitely not, the only person she would have allowed in is her long-time friend, Nellie Gibson, they go back a long way, friends since school days they were. Nellie always kept an eye out for mother she lived at number 8 just across from mother at 5 Leaming Avenue, Waterlooville, in Portsmouth.'

*

Smyth and Devon park a few doors down from Nellie Gibson's address.

'Boss, I get the feeling that old Nellie is the Neighbourhood Watch type, especially as I can see someone peering through the nets at number 8.'

'Yep, I can feel her eyes on us too! Let's go pay her a visit, Devon.'

They cross the road and knock on the door of number 8. A dog starts to bark from within as Nellie shouts out.

'Hold on, hold on I'm coming!'

The barking and yapping intensifies as the door half opens and Nellie peers out.'

'Can I help you dearies?' She looks back over her shoulder and shouts a command at the dog.

'Pearl stop it, shut up! Sorry about that Ladies but she does go on.'

'Nellie isn't it?'

'Yes, yes, are you here to tell me I've won the post code lottery?'

'Sorry to disappoint but unfortunately Nellie no.'

'Oh what a shame, what a shame maybe next time, hey.'

'I'm Detective Inspector Smyth,' she shows Nellie her ID card. 'And this is my colleague Officer Devon, do you mind if we step inside and have a little chat with you?'

'No, no not at all, I'm glad of the company, I'm a bit hard of hearing I'm afraid, but I'll do my best. Oh and take no notice of Pearl, she does bark an awful lot especially at strangers, well come to think of it, anyone. She'll soon settle in her basket, that's where she keeps her favourite squeaky toy you know, but sometimes, for a quiet life, I remove the squeak,' She shouts 'Basket, Pearl, to your basket!' Pearl, a Chihuahua, skulks away.

'There's a good girl. Right now ladies, where were we, oh yes come in, come in'

Nellie shows them into the front room where Pearl lies in her basket quietly chewing on her silent toy.

'Ladies would you like a cup of tea and a biscuit?'

'No thank you Nellie.'

'Now dearies, how can I be of assistance? Please sit, sit.'

'Officer Devon will be taking down notes but it's not something to worry yourself about, it's normal procedure.'

'Oh, this is so exciting,'

'Well Nellie, we understand that you and Ida had been very close friends for a very long time. And we are very sorry for your loss it must have been a great wrench for you.'

'Sorry, but can you speak a bit slower and a bit louder dearie, it's these old ears of mine. Oh I've tried wearing hearing aids, but no good I'm afraid, they leave me with itchy ears and all those damn screeching noise, that come from them when I'm trying to put them in, that's not the worst of it mind the worst is when the batteries go dead half way through a conversation, anyway, go ahead dearies.'

'We understand that you and Ida were very close friends, we are very sorry for your loss it must have been a great wrench for you.'

76

'Yes it was dearie, terrible, terrible, I do miss her, no, it's not been the same since poor old Ida, well, you know, passed on.'

'Nellie did Ida tell you about any visitors she may have had or ones you may have seen and didn't know of?'

'No not really, no, only that that lovely young man of course.'

'What young man was that Nellie?'

'You know, the young man who spoke at Ida's husband's funeral service, she referred to him as a celebrant. Yes that's right, celebrant, well at least I think that's what she called him. He had such a lovely way with words; very well spoken and nicely dressed too, yes very smart. You don't get many young people dressing like that nowadays, it's normally those ripped jeans and T-shirt. Ida had told me on many occasions that she was ever so pleased with him and how well he conducted Harry's funeral service.'

'Do you remember his name, the celebrant that is, the person who Ida was so pleased with?'

'Give me a minute will you, my mind is not as sharp as it used to be. I used to work in a betting office and I tell you, you needed your wits about you when doing that a job like that. Life, it all goes downhill after seventy you know and that was ten years ago. Yes, you were asking about his name…I remember now, yes of course, Peter North that's his name. Peter North.'

'Well done for remembering, so, when did you last see this Peter North?'

'Let me see, he came to visit Ida on two occasions about Harry's funeral service, now I know that because I was there during his first visit. It was then he suggested that only he and Ida should meet during his follow up visit. Now, I must admit, I did feel a bit put out by that but I understood they needed to discuss things further, discuss more private matters. Now the next time I saw him was at Harry's funeral service. Then about a month later and that must have been the last time I saw him. By chance I saw Ida letting him in to hers, he seemed to be in there forever, not that I was watching you understand.'

'Nellie I want you to think about this really carefully, did Ida mention anything, to you about this visit?'

'No, she never mentioned it, not in the slightest, now, that's not like Ida, but I didn't want to pry you see, I never pry, oh no, oh no, I never pry.'

'Did she seem upset in any way?'

'No, quite the opposite, she somehow seemed pleased with herself, now are you sure wouldn't like a cup of tea? I have biscuits of all varieties.'

'No thank you and you are quite sure that the celebrant's name is Peter North and that he was the same person who called in on Ida sometime after the funeral service?'

'Oh yes dearie the same, he's such a lovely man,' she holds up a pack of biscuits 'McVities anyone?'

*

As DI Smyth and Officer Devon leave Nellie's they notice Mr James Summers standing at the front door of his mother's house. He quietly calls out to them and beckons them across. Smyth and Devon cross the road to see what he wants.

'Pssst, excuse me officers, can I have a quick word. Just saw you leaving Nellie's, you didn't mention anything to her about, well you know, the missing money did you?'

'Mr Summers we just had an informal chat with her just in case she had seen or heard anything that may help us in our inquiries.'

'And?'

'And what Mr Summers?'

'Did she have anything to say?'

'As you're here Mr Summers, I would like to ask a few questions myself just so I can get an overall picture, fill in the blanks, you know.'

'Of course, yes of course.'

'Your father's funeral service, which undertakers did you use?'

'We organised it through Mr Clifton, the manager of J.C. Funeral Services, however, we will be going through a different

78

funeral director for mother's funeral service and that's only because she had a pre-arranged funeral plan with them, otherwise it would have been J.C. Funeral Services again . Like my father my mother was not the religious type, not everyone is you know, so I imagine we will be dealing with a celebrant, albeit a different one from father's, although I must say father's one was excellent.'

'Do you recall the celebrant's name, the one who officiated at your father's service?'

'Well, it's funny you should ask that, it was only yesterday that I was looking through father's 'Order of Service', you couldn't have wished for a better sending off, it was beautiful, the celebrant's name is printed on the cover, it's Peter North, I'll go and get it and show you if you want'

'That won't be necessary. Well, thank you Mr Summers. I will be in contact with you soon.'

Across the road at number 8 the curtains twitched

Before driving away DI Smyth looks across at Devon.

'Let's go pay J. C. Funerals a visit, Devon. Oh and as a precaution, in case old J.C. is in on it, well, just play along will you! A little white lie won't go amiss.'

'Sure, always prepared to learn new investigative techniques boss.'

'Devon, you know what? You'll go a long way.'

Chapter 16

DI Smyth and Officer Devon enter J.C Funeral Services and make their way to where receptionist Ruth Cumberland is sat busying herself at her desk, having just ended a phone call. She stands and introduces herself.

'Good morning ladies my name is Ruth Cumberland, Mr Clifton's receptionist, how can I be of assistance?'

'Good morning Ruth, is it possible to speak to Mr Clifton?'

'Of course, who shall I say wants him?'

'It's a confidential matter.'

'Oh, of course, I won't be a moment. If you would like to take a seat please do so.'

They remain standing as Ruth, feeling put out that her position has been undermined, disappears behind the red crushed velvet curtains that hang at the rear of reception. Several minutes later, she reappears.

'James, I mean, Mr Clifton, will be with you shortly.'

From behind her desk she produces a grey miniature watering can and starts to attend to the flower arrangements that adorn the waiting room. From behind the curtains James Clifton makes his entrance.

'Good morning ladies, James Clifton, Manager and funeral director of this establishment, at your service. My receptionist Ruth has informed me that you would like to speak with me concerning a confidential matter, all sounds rather mysterious I must say, so here I am, put me out of my misery!'

'Mr Clifton, it's nothing to worry about sir I'm....'

'My dear lady, if there is one thing I do not do is worry as it interferes with one's sleep and overall feeling of wellbeing.'

'Well I'm glad to hear that. I'm Detective Inspector Smyth and this is Officer Devon. The Health and Safety Executive has asked us to do what is known as a drop-in check whereby on occasions we visit premises on their behalf, think of it as a sort of job share.'

'A job share you say DI Smyth.'

'I know what you're thinking sir and you would be right, it's a bit of overkill sending us when normally it would be a Health and Safety inspector, as I said, we happen to be in the area and they are short staffed and very busy, apparently.'

'Oh I see my dear lady, although, I'm just finding it rather difficult to imagine a Health and Safety officer attending a murder scene. Now that would be interesting. Well, I can assure both you ladies these premises comply fully with all Health and Safety standards meeting all the regulations. But we will be able to talk more privately in my office and it is where I keep my paperwork. Please, follow me.'

Smyth and Devon follow Clifton behind the curtains into a dimly lit corridor. They walk towards a lit neon exit sign situated above a doorway leading them into the rear of a busy garage, its parking area full of various styles and makes of grey and black Hearses. Having weaved their way between the parked cars they are then led across a small cobblestone courtyard before coming to a halt outside a single level red brick building. On its door there is a sign saying 'Manager Private'. Inside the red brick building Smyth and Devon are surprised at how big an open space it is and yet, in one corner, there is only one desk, a filing cabinet and seven chairs which are arranged in a semi-circle, each with its own side table containing bottled water and a glass. Facing the semicircle of chairs is the manager's, a sumptuous leather chair.

'Welcome to the hub of my operation, please take a seat.' With a dramatic wave of his hand Clifton directs Smyth and Devon to two of the seven chairs, whilst he sits in the Manager's.

'Please excuse the seating arrangement only we had a team meeting earlier this morning. Well, here we are then, oh, I warn you, before you start, it has been a very strange few days for me, indeed, very strange, I may seem at times distracted .'

'Excuse me for asking Mr Clifton but why do you say that sir, you know, about it being a strange few days, in what way?'

He sighs, 'Well honestly, where do I begin, it was only yesterday when a man came in and asked me if I knew the whereabouts, or have the contact number of a particular celebrant who works for me. I asked him why, his reply was so he could arrange a self-styled funeral service for his late mother thus cutting out the middle man. Honestly, I mean the flipping cheek of it all! This is a job for professionals and professionals only not any old riffraff.'

'Just out of interest, did he give his name?'

'Ha, as if I could forget, he referred to himself simply as Mayfair. I enquired into his full name but he just repeated, in a very aggressive manner I might add, Mayfair. He stood, in reception, just staring at me, waiting for a reply. His whole demeanour started to change before my very eyes and for the worse I can tell you, it made me feel very uncomfortable indeed so uncomfortable my legs started to shake. I mean, the ignorant so and so. No doubt the rough type if you ask me.'

'Can you describe him?'

'Describe him! I've been having nightmares thinking about him. Afro-Caribbean I would say, about six-foot five, well-kept, wearing a dark blue suit and expensive shoes.'

'Shoes, so you noticed his shoes'

'Oh yes, especially when someone is wearing shoes that are of handmade quality, of course I do, it says something about that person ....well, normally it does. He spoke in a London accent, east of the river I suspect. The size of his hands, well, they resembled shovels they were so big. I really should invest in CCTV, but then you wouldn't expect that type of clientele in a place such as this would you,'

'And did you?'

'Did I what young lady?'

'Put him in contact with the celebrant he asked for.'

'Well yes. I mean, after a stare like that I felt obliged to. Oh no, you wouldn't want to argue with someone like that I can tell you.'

'And who is this celebrant he asked for?'

'Ask! It sounded more like demanded. He specifically wanted Peter, Peter North, who by the way is my most reliable and respected celebrant specialising in non-religious services, he's such a love. So yes, I gave him Peter. Afterwards I worried so much, you know hoping I had done the right thing because it's something I would never ever do normally, give out information regarding my celebrants that is.'

'What do you mean you gave him Peter North, Mr Clifton?'

'I told him where he could find him.'

'And where was that?'

'I told him that Peter generally sets up office in The Swan. Naughty of him I know, but he does. It is something I tend to overlook because it does not reflect in anyway on this establishment I mean really, who's to know. And after all, he does work as a freelancer, celebrants normally do you know.'

'When you say The Swan do you mean the public house just along the High Street from here?'

'Yes I do, mind you, you wouldn't catch me in there, oh no, it has a bit of a rough reputation you see. Although, all credit due I have heard it has recently had a re-fit, sad though…'

'What is?'

'That, they can't do the same to the clientele. As for me of course, I prefer a more select establishment a more congenial atmosphere, for instance I…'

'So out of interest, how well do you know this Peter North?'

'Well he introduced himself to me at these premises, let me see, about three getting on for four years ago. A very good looking chap and very well spoken, he told me he had lots of experience as a celebrant and what he would be expected to be paid. I found his rate to be quite reasonable. What really swung it in his favour was when he said he would consider it an honour to be out there representing J.C. Funeral Services. So, I gave him the opportunity to prove himself, which is always a worrying time for us funeral directors, our reputations are on the line you see, in this profession you are only as good as your last funeral, but he came through with flying colours. The family were ever so pleased with him. The rest as they say is history.'

'So, over these past years there have been no complaints about his conduct?'

'No not one iota.'

'Absolutely fascinating, don't you find it fascinating Devon?'

'I do boss, yes, how it all works, the funeral business that is.'

'Bear with me Mr Clifton, using Peter as an example, what background checks would you have made before employing him, you know checking things like his work history and criminal record if any?'

'Look, we tend to find those sorts of things are not necessary as we don't actually employ celebrants they work for us but we don't employ them as such. If someone can do the job competently then they are taken on. The many who claim to be celebrants and who are really not up to the job don't last. It's quite a responsibility being a celebrant not many people realise that. A celebrant often visits frail elderly people, who are left on their own due their partner's death. They visit families who have lost children, mothers and fathers and other family members. It's not easy for the celebrant or the family but it's a job that has to been done.'

'Mr Clifton, yes I am fully aware that Celebrants need to have access to families and individuals who are at a highly vulnerable time of their lives, I've experienced it myself when my father died and the support I got from the Celebrant was excellent, however here you are telling me that no background checks are ever made on such people, doesn't that worry you? Christ that's an accident just waiting to happen if ever there was one. When dealing with the vulnerable, employees are required by law, to undergo a DBS check. Why should Celebrants be any different?'

'Look, you have a valid point but I have no knowledge of background checks ever being made on anyone in this job, but that's down to the individual company I suppose. And there have been no problems up to now not with this establishment I can tell you that now.'

'Are you certain of that Mr Clifton? Still, I find the whole thing highly disturbing, it seriously needs looking into. Make a note of that Devon.'

'Beat you to it boss,'

Clifford feels highly agitated 'Excuse me you seem to have an unhealthy interest in Peter North and the integrity of this establishment?'

'I can assure you Mr Clifton that I have no interest whatsoever who you choose to work for you. I apologise, I guess with wearing so many different hats, professionally that is, I sometimes I find it hard to differentiate between them all, I do apologise.'

'I understand. Yes, that must be problematic, I apologise for my outburst.'

DI Smyth's radio starts to bleep. 'It would seem that we are wanted back at the station. Well sir, we have got to go so thank you for your time, it's been a pleasure meeting you.'

'But you haven't looked around the premises yet or even checked my certification.'

'I'm sure Health and Safety will be in touch.'

As Smyth and Devon step outside on to the busy High Street they are captured in the camera lens of the DCD9 undercover surveillance team.

'Nice one boss, I mean, the bleeping, to get us out of there. You took him to task over the DBS Service and I don't blame you'

'Yes, I was beginning to dig myself a deep hole back there. But I was so incensed that DBS checks were not being made which is disturbing and potentially dangerous. We'll have to pass it on to those in the know. Anyway Devon, fancy a drink! I've heard The Swan serve a tasty pint and it's where we might find us a Celebrant. We'll walk it as we are on the High Street and practically there.'

A flummoxed James Clifton makes an internal call to reception.

'Ruth.'

'Yes James.'

'Eye mask and gin bottle please Ruth I'm in need of a very large stiff drink and a dark room. If anyone wants me I'm out.'

'Didn't go well then?'

'Well, they were no more interested in Health and Safety than I am straight, but what the hell.'

Chapter 17

The SCD9 Special Unit surveillance team patch images of two unknowns entering and leaving J.C. Funeral Services across to DI Guilford. From her desk she signals over to Grant who is sat at his desk to join her.

'Look Paul, I've just received incoming intel from the surveillance team at J.C. Funeral Services, its images of two unknown females. The vehicle they parked-up in is being run through the system now.'

As they study the images of the two unknowns Grant is positive that he recognises one of them.

'Fay I rec…'

'Bloody hell Paul, sorry mate but take a look at this, the trace on the car has come up as belonging to the Force.'

'And you know what Fay, I was just about to say I'm sure I recognise one of these women, yes it's err, what's her name, come on, come on, what is it, yes, Helen Smyth, it's Helen Smyth she's a DI from Fraud.'

'What! Are you sure?'

'I'm sure alright. We met during a police conference. The Home Secretary was giving a lecture on sharing information, crime results, cut backs and all that shit. We bumped into each other in the canteen and started chatting. That's when she introduced herself. It's her Fay, no mistaking, I never forget a face.'

'Now, what the fuck is Fraud doing at J.C. Funerals?'

Another email pings on Guilford's lap top.

'Listen to this, it reads, unknown male identified as a private detective who goes by the name of John Mayfair.' Grant bangs his fist on the desk.

'Fay, we need to get an angle on this and bloody quick.'

Guilford dials extension 10. 'Ma'am, DI Fay Guilford, I need to see you ASAP, it's a matter of urgency.'

'Come straight up.'

Grant and Guilford knock on Detective Chief Inspector Edinburgh's office door and walk in.

'Ok you two talk to me.'

'Ma'am, Operation 'Solo 1' is in danger of being severely compromised. One of two female unknowns entering and leaving the premises of J.C. Funeral Services has been identified as a DI from the Fraud Squad. There was another unknown with her but as yet unidentified. Add to that, a male has been identified as Private Detective John Mayfair. It's becoming a circus and we need to know what's going on.'

'I agree I'll get straight on to Fraud to see what I can find out, meanwhile see what you can find out about the Private Detective.'

'Yes Ma'am.'

'I'm going to arrange an urgent team briefing, warn the others will you.'

'Yes Ma'am.'

Chapter 18

Mayfair enters the Swan Public House and makes his way to the bar. Whilst waiting to be served he scans the room looking for someone who fits the description that was given to him by Zara Maxwell which was of a Hugh Jackman look alike. Having earlier Googled an image of Hugh Jackman, Mayfair was certain that no one in the bar bore the slightest resemblance.

Looking across the bar into the lounge, Mayfair's attention is drawn to someone at one of the tables who is busying himself typing on a laptop, who to his amazement, actually did fit the description.

Mia is stood behind the bar polishing glasses.

'Be with you soon Mr, just on my last glass.'

'No sweat love, I'm in no rush. Nice place, had it done-up recently, I can still smell the paint and the flooring looks new.'

'Yep, looks much better now, you should have seen it before, it was well past its sell by date. You're not a regular in here are you? Only I have a good memory for faces and names, it helps me in this job no end, to be quite honest, if you don't mind and no offence, we don't get many of well you know your type, black people, no we don't get many in here, God knows why, but we don't. We all share the same planet why not the same pubs.'

'Well, maybe, just maybe I'm the first of many! Look out us black folk are on our way!' He thinks the gall of the racist bitch.

'You know what, I can normally tell what a customer is drinking and have it on this bar before they reach it having walked through those doors. Well in most cases anyway. I can't seem to read you though.'

Mayfair points through into the lounge. 'Ok then Mystic Meg, what's he drinking?'

She turns to see who he means.

'Who?'

'Him through there with all that paperwork on the table, what's he drinking?'

'Well, that's easy, he comes here most days. It's his office, well that's what he calls it, it's a bit of a running joke around here. He drinks lager.'

'Why that is amazing! If not a bit unfair as he is a regular and you've not long served him by the looks of it. Next you'll be telling me you can guess his name! Although I feel you already know it!'

'Well actually I do, it's Peter.'

'Brilliant! How do you do it! Go on then, no forget it, it would be pushing your mystic powers too far.'

'What would? No it wouldn't, go on, ask me?'

'Ok then, now this one you won't know, what does Peter there do as a job?' 'He's one of those celebrant types who speak at funerals, a bit creepy don't you think? I mean talking about the dead and in front of all those people too.'

'Mia you should be polishing crystal balls not glasses!'

'Still, I think it's creepy.'

'Mind you, if what he's doing helps people get over their loss, why not. By the way, what's your name young lady?'

She puts down the tea towel and holds out a hand to shake Mayfair's. He declines the offer.

'Mia's the name, pleased to meet you and what's yours?

'My name, well, that's top secret.'

'So what are you drinking Mr Mystery Man?'

'A pint of lager please Mia, no make that two pints.'

While Mia is pouring out two pints of lager, Mayfair, to confirm he has his man, dials the number Zara Maxwell gave him. He hears it ringing and sees the man sitting in the lounge answer. Mayfair cuts the call.

'There you go, that'll be £8, 60.'

'Here's £10, keep the change.'

With a pint in each hand Mayfair makes his way into the lounge and stands at the table North is sitting at. North stops typing and looks up.

'This tables taken.'

'Nonsense, I've got you a pint in.'

Avoiding the laptop and paperwork, Mayfair slides one of the pints of lager over to North who looks across at Mia. She shrugs her shoulders, smiles and carries on polishing more glasses.

'Peter? I am right aren't I? You are Peter North the celebrant?'

'How can I help you Mister?'

Mayfair pulls up a chair.

'Mayfair's the name, not that that's going to mean anything to you.'

He pulls his chair up closer to North.

'Look at this place, you seem to have a nice thing going on here my friend, pretty young barmaid, drinks on tap, it's nice and warm no over-heads and all for the cost of a pint, man you got it sussed. Yes sir you got it sussed alright.'

'Like I said, whatever your name, this tables taken, you're not welcome.'

'Well, I'm not sure how to say this without it sounding too dramatic or me coming across as a complete mad man. But believe me what I am about I say is with the gravest of conviction and importance, you must steel yourself and do as I say.' North thinks what the fuck is this nutter on about.

'Do what you say! Oh sure and what's that?'

'Without making a scene, gather up the paperwork, close down the laptop and come with me, we're going for a drive.'

'Is this your fucking way of picking up men? You sweet talking bastard look, I'm not into that sort of thing so fuck off and try the toilets you'll get more luck in there.'

North feels something sharp pressing into his side, he looks down and sees part of a blade.

'Ah, Peter, I'm not gay, no, no, no, all I want is a talk with you in private but you don't seem to want that. The knife, well, that's there to let you know I'm a serious bitch who means business.'

North thinks, I want to know what this fucker wants me for, so play along for the time being.

90

'Okay, keep it under control will you mate. It's going to take a few minutes.'

Mayfair takes a gulp of his lager.

'Good, compliance is a lovely thing. As a matter of interest do you know why I favour this type of weapon, the knife that is?'

'Look mate, whoever the fuck you are, I really couldn't give a shit?' I could turn that on you and gut you here and now, you black fuck.

'Oh don't be like that Peter, I do enjoy a bit of chit-chat now and again, finish your lager while I explain. Well it's what is known as a commando knife. It pierces under minimal force and its specially designed cambered blade stops bodily fats and fluids sucking on to it thus making it easier to extract.'

North thinks, you'll be teaching me to suck eggs next, you big fuck.

'A well thought out design, in fact genius,' He applies more pressure with the knife. 'Now, as I was saying, close your laptop, gather up all your papers, we're leaving, now.'

North thinks, I could take this fucker, but not now, not here.

*

Having walked from JC Funeral Services DI Smyth and Officer Devon arrive at The Swan. As they approach the entrance through the thick coloured glass panelled doors Devon can make out two figures approaching from within, presumably on their way out. She jumps one step ahead of Smyth, pulls open one of the doors and holds it open allowing the two men to make their exit.

'Please, after you gentlemen.' She says with a wave of her hand.

Mayfair smiles back. 'Why thank you young lady, you both have yourselves a nice day now.'

Smyth and Devon enter and make their way to the bar. Referring to the two men who had just left, Devon jokes. 'I didn't like the look of your one boss.' They laugh.

Mia is busying herself at the bar. 'Hi Ladies, what's your pleasure? Let me guess, two G&Ts.'

'Actually we're looking for someone who we believe is one of your regulars, hoping one of the bar staff would be able to point him out for us.'

'This is the second mystery of the day! And as you can see I'm bar staff so go on then, give me the name.'

'Peter North, have you seen him or better still is he here?'

'Well, this must be his lucky day! I'm Mia by the way. First he gets bought a pint by a complete stranger, then you two turn up! Like I said, the second mystery of the day!'

'So, is he here then?'

'Ok love, hold on to your horses,' she looks through to the lounge. 'Yes he's here alright,' She points. 'He's through there with….well that's odd, he was there a second ago, maybe he's gone to the loo, no, hold on love, looks like the table he refers to as his office, is clear of all of his things. It seems you two must have just missed him. Maybe he had business with that bloke, the mystery man I told you about the one who bought him the drink!'

Smyth and Devon look at each other in disbelief at what may have just happened.

'Fuck boss,' They both run outside to the carpark. Mia rushes from behind the bar and follows. 'Everything ok out here ladies? You can't just go running through the place it'll upset the customers.'

'Sorry Mia, no, I mean yes, we were hoping to have a few words with him.'

'Who?'

'Peter North of course.'

Mia points to a silver Jaguar 4x4 parked in the carpark.

'Well ladies, he can't have gone far 'cos his car is still here. Maybe he took off with that bloke after all. Could be something to do with the line of work he's in, after all he uses this pub as if it were his office. Anyway, have a nice day ladies I've got customers to serve, ciao. Oh, and if you do manage to see him, give him my love. Mia's the name, just in case you forgot.'

Officer Devon notes the registration number of North's Jag.

'Boss, I'm sorry, had I realised I...Fuck!
'Drop it Devon we both screwed up. Let's go.'

Chapter 19

Mayfair drives into the grounds of Portsmouth Crematorium and parks in a spot next to its well-maintained gardens in an area which is slightly hidden under the shadows of a row of trees. He pushes the central locking button on the dashboard, the mechanism kicks in and secures the door from being opened, he partly lowers his and the passenger window.

'Man, it is so peaceful here and the smell of all that freshly cut grass, sweet I tell you, sweet. But what am I saying; you would know this of course, you must come here often in your line of business. I personally don't agree with all this burning of bodies shit. I know it's nowhere near the same but I can't help being reminded of what I read about the times way back when Henry VIII would put people to the stake, man that was a nasty business.'

North thinks, this guy talks a load of shit. 'OK Mayfair, enough of the history lesson, and by the way it's nothing like the way you put it, the people they cremate here are already dead. So come on what's the crack, what the fuck is this all about and why is it so important that you found it necessary to drive us here of all places?'

'Well that depends on you.'

'On me, what the fuck are you on about.'

'You know a Mrs Zara Maxwell, right?'

'In passing, why do you ask?'

North is caught off guard as Mayfair, using a reverse hand punch, hits him in the face. Jerking back then forward North cups his bleeding face in both hands, he doesn't retaliate. Mayfair is surprised how well North takes the blow.

'Unlock this door and get out of the car now, I'll kick your black fucking balls in you black fuck.'

'Peter, do you know a Zara Maxwell?

Still cupping his mouth and nose with his hands North's words are muffled. 'I'll kill you, you fucking bastard.'

'What was that Peter,, I can't hear you?'

'Fuck you! Unlock these doors'

'Now did you fuck Mrs Zara Maxwell over for the amount of £30,000?'

Mayfair, using an outstretched left arm attempts to press the side of North's face against the passenger side window. North grabs hold of Mayfair's fingers and thumb and bends them back. Another centimetre and they would break.

Mayfair releases, pulling back in pain.

'Shit. Fuck you man, you nearly broke my fingers.'

North starts to laugh as he slumps back into his seat, blood trickles from his lips and nose as he rest his head on the headrest. There is a slight swelling forming over his left eye.

'Pain, fucking hell Mayfair you don't know what pain is, open these fucking doors and I'll give you a real taste of it.'

'Peter North, you're a strange one that's for sure.'

Mayfair reaches over to the back seat, North grabs hold of his arm. 'Relax man, don't you go breaking my arm, I'm just reaching for a box of tissues.'

'Look man we are both men of the world so let's cool it. Here, have some of these tissues and don't you worry about getting blood on my seat, as you can see it's well covered with polythene, especially for occasions such as this. Can you just wipe that spot of blood off your window, thanks man, the cost of valeting a vehicle these days can be extortionate, do you agree?'

'What! Oh yeah, yeah, they're thieving bastards alright you crazy fuck!'

Mayfair opens both windows all the way down.

'Get some of that sweet fresh air into your lungs and clean yourself up, there's a mirror behind the sun visor and more tissues, even a comb if you need one, in the dash. Look man, I am good at heart, a little crazy, a bit like you I think. I would like to make a suggestion, you ok with that?

'Well, that fucking depends on…...'

'I suggest we get a little truce going on here. Look man if Maxwell hadn't come to me, she would have eventually gone to the boys in blue and then you really would have been in the shit. I'm just here representing my client Mrs Maxwell so screw all the others you have fucked over or are about to fuck over. I suggest that we make Mrs Maxwell a very happy woman by returning her £30,000. And you know what for my troubles, I suggest, let me think, no, I can't decide. How much do you think you should pay me as a bonus for all my troubles and to forget that you ever existed? After all, like I said, my intentions are not to stop you doing your thing man. If I could do that thing you do, that celebrant thing I would do it myself. Try seeing it this way, as well as Maxwell getting her money back, you too have an interest in this and that's stopping you being busted by the police. So, back to my question how much do you think you should pay me as a bonus for all my troubles and to forget that you ever existed? That's after you've paid up of course.'

'I've no fucking idea, £3,000, £5,000?' Mayfair cautiously places his left hand firmly on North's knee. North restrains himself from breaking Mayfair's fingers and smashing his head into the steering wheel.

'Now I think you can do better than that, don't you?'

'Number one, remove your fucking hand off of my knee and number two, I really don't give a fuck what you're talking about but to keep the peace, £10,000? Like I said I don't really give a fuck!'

'BINGO! Man you're cool. Doesn't The Lord say Blessed are those who help themselves? By the way man how's the face?'

'Could be better but you know what, I'll get over it?'

'Like I said earlier, there's something about you, something that just don't add up. Anyway listen. It's only fair that I give you 48 hours to sort out the money side of things, cash only of course. I will contact you nearer the time then we can put all of this behind us. Now I would like you to consider that as being a reasonable request.'

'And that will be the end of it?'

'Yes, I will be happy, Mrs Maxwell will be happy and with no police involvement, you can just carry on doing what makes you happy and that's fucking over all those sad women.'

'Okay Mayfair, let's roll with it,' He thinks, better this than have to eliminate this black fucker and have Maxwell eventually report me to the police.

'Excellent, now where can I drop you off?'

'Back at The Swan, I'm parked up there.'

'Not that silver 4X4 Jag with tinted windows, I've always wanted tinted windows, the darker the better. I think they're really cool, but then, I've always wanted a Jag too!'

'It's no big deal.'

'Are you fucking with me man, it's a great car? Much better than this pile of shit, won't be long before it's in junk yard heaven, maybe you could say a few words when that time comes, you know being a celebrant and all. This shit you're doing man, the celebrant thing. How did you get into it?'

'I took the good advice of an old acquaintance of mine. It suits my needs.'

'Yeah, let me guess what's driving those needs of yours, your need for pussy and money but I recon it goes deeper than that, I get the impression you enjoy inflicting as much psychological damage on your victims as you can. I mean what is it really all about man? Look at me for instance, when it calls for it, in my line of business, I can be a mean motherfucker and when it's over and done with it's over and done with, bones mend, cuts heal, end of, these are the rules we live by on the street but what you do I've never come it across before. It's subtle yet dangerous it's a scam but not a scam, yes you make money but you operate at another level where there aren't any rules. You play with people's lives at the same time as destroying them.'

'Look Mayfair I have my demons, we all do, let's leave it at that.'

Chapter 20

Mia sees North walk inside the Swan and sit at his normal seat in the lounge. As soon as she finishing serving customers' with a tray of drinks she goes over to him.

'Crikey! What's happened to you?'

'Don't ask, could have been worse, for the other guy that is. I guess it was his lucky day. Some paracetamol please and a pint to wash them down with oh and Mia be a love,' he holds his jaw. 'Wrap some ice in a T-towel will you.'

'Sure, although paracetamol taken with water would do you a lot better but you're the boss!'

'Please Mia, just get it. Apart from my mouth killing me, my next service is tomorrow and this swelling needs to go down or I'll be speaking like I've just come from the dentist.'

The ringtone on North's mobile sounds. He thinks, for fuck sake what now.

'You'll have to excuse me Mia I've got to take this.'

'Ok, I'll come back in a few minutes with your medical order!'

'And don't forget the T-towel and ice.'

'Your wish is my command,' she bows before walking away.

North takes the call. 'Peter its James from J.C. Funeral Services. It's Ruth's half-day today so reception duties are yet another one of my jobs. Would you be able to take on a service for me next Monday morning at 9.45? Only the family have asked for you because you did such a good service for their late Uncle.'

'That's kind of them. I haven't got my diary with me at the moment James but thinking ahead I am sure that will be fine. If you email me the details I will be in contact with the family, then as soon as I have visited them I will let you know the order of service and their choice of music if any.'

'They are a lovely family who have just lost their stepfather the contact name is a Mrs Helen Martin. Excellent, one more thing while I've got you, just checking that you have received the information Ruth emailed you regarding Mr Dennis Forrester's funeral service?'

'Yes I have thank you James. By the way, how have you been keeping?'

'My dear man you wouldn't believe what's been going on here of late. You know, I feel something is in the air but I can't quite put my finger on it. It's as if the whole world has gone completely mad. Anyway thank you Peter love, look after yourself. Oh by the way before you go, is everything ok with you? It's just that…'

'I'm good thanks, couldn't be better. Sorry James what was it you were about to say?'

'Oh nothing, it's ok, it's just me being a daft old gay I suppose. Not to worry love, hear from you soon.'

Chapter 21

At the SCD9 Special Unit, Detective Chief Inspector Edinburgh calls a meeting with Guilford and Grant.

'I have been in contact with Fraud and had quite a conversation. It transpires that the reason their DI and one of their Officers have been seen at the premises of J.C. Funeral Services is due to the fact that they are making inquiries into someone who goes by the name of Peter North who has allegedly defrauded a family, stroke families, out of thousands of pounds.

'Hold on Ma'am! Did you say Peter North, the celebrant Peter North?'

'Yes that's right it was mentioned during our conversation that North is a celebrant.'

Guilford and Grant look at each other in disbelief.

'Ma'am, I don't believe this, this is great news and it's the breakthrough we've been looking for. We need to talk to him ASAP. Yes he could be exactly what we are looking for.'

'Explain to me how this Peter North who's a celebrant can be of help to us.'

'Ok Ma'am, the Funeral Director at J.C. Funeral Services told Paul that a celebrant who goes by the name of Peter North will be officiating at the Forrester's funeral service and that he will be visiting Mrs Forrester in order to make arrangements for the funeral service. Now, if Fraud is interested in Peter North he must have been a naughty boy. If we can get to him first and inform him of Fraud's intentions he might want a way out. We can give him that way out by offering him a deal, he helps us and we help him. Ma'am, we need to get to him first. We can't let a golden opportunity as good as this slip by.'

'Well I can tell you now Fraud is not going to like it. You do know that don't you.'

'Ma'am, if we can pick him up before they do then officially he's ours. Paul.'

'Yes Ma'am, Fraud can still have their man, just a bit later!'

'Well it definitely is the break we've been looking for. Actually, I don't know why I'm hesitating, go bring him in. Guess I'll be taking a lot of flak over this but that's what I get paid for.'

*

From inside his car, DS Grant calls an old associate of his, Tony Elms, a DI who works in the Serious Fraud Squad.

'Hi, mate it's Paul. Paul Grant,'

'Oh hi Paul, how's it swinging?'

'Yeah it's all good mate, all good. How are Pamela and the kids?'

'Well you know what it's like, always a strain on the old wallet! And these new shifts they've got us working, well it don't help with matrimonial matters that's for sure.'

'Look mate, I'm going to have to cut to the chase and be up front with you, I'm working on something big and I need some inside info.'

'So what's going down?'

'There's this guy, who is about to be picked up by you lot, nothing proven on him yet mind, but I need him before you lot get their hands on him. I can't go into too much detail right now but it could mean the difference between a seven month operation succeeding or going tits-up, big time. I know it's a big ask mate but…'

'Let's have it then.'

'Well the guy in question is Peter North. He works as a celebrant, one of those people who speak at funeral services, the name James Clifton of J.C. Funeral Services may be of some help, North's done some work for him. Tony I need to know his whereabouts and anything and everything you have on this Peter North guy because we need to have a bargaining chip to get this asshole to want to make a deal. You know how it goes.'

'Well I've got a heavy workload on at the moment. How soon do you want it?'

'Sorry mate but it's like I say, I need it as though it was yesterday.'

'I'll do my best. The name Peter North doesn't ring a bell but there's a possibility his file has been handed over to a unit that has recently been set up.'

'It wouldn't be the new Cold Case Fraud Unit I've heard about would it?'

'That's the one.'

'In that case Tony, I do have a name for you, Helen Smyth, DI Helen Smyth.'

'Helen, yes I know her, she one of ours alright, we have some history between us so leave it with me mate.'

*

DI Smyth and Officer Devon have returned to their office, waiting for them are officers Baines and Khair.

'Ok, so, we paid a visit to Mr James Summers, the son of Ida Summers, he is convinced that his mother has been a victim of fraud to the amount of £15,000 which was apparently discovered after he had been through her accounts. We also paid a visit to one of her neighbours, best friend Nellie Clarke. Devon, take the lead.'

'Thanks Boss, well, Nellie came up with some useful information. She alleges she did recognise a man by the name of Peter North. He officiated at Ida's husband's funeral service and was seen by Nellie paying Ida a visit soon after the funeral service.'

'Thank you Devon. We paid J.C. Funeral Services a visit and spoke to the owner manager a Mr James Clifton. Now we had every reason to believe that if Peter North is our man then Clifton might be involved too, but having spoken to him I doubt it very much. However, we'll keep an open mind on that one. It would seem that North is a freelancer working as a celebrant for different funeral establishments. It has also come to light that North and others in the same line of work do not necessarily undergo DBS checks. Now, that's an open cheque for any scammer, con-man. Devon will be informing the appropriate authorities.'

'It seems to be common knowledge that he uses The Swan public house as his office. Apparently he can often be seen in the lounge on his phone and working away on his laptop. Devon and I went there on the off chance of him being there but as luck would have it we just missed him.'

Devon looks down sheepishly.

*

DI Tony Elms from the Fraud Squad contacts the Cold Case unit and speaks to DI Helen Smyth.

'Hi, Helen this is Tony, Tony Elms.'

'Oh hi Tony, long-time no see.'

'It's these long bloody hours we're expected to work, so nothing personal you understand.'

'Yeah, I must admit my hours feel like 24/7 since I took lead role over here.'

'So, how's it going?'

'Early days yet but yeah ok, I take it this is not an informal call?'

'Don't be like that Helen, we're still good with one another aren't we? I mean as far as friends go anyway. I'm always here in case you need a chat or a helping hand. For instance, the case we recently sent over, was it any help to your inquiries?'

'Sorry Tony, yes it was. I now have a leading suspect. Just about to run his plates through the PNC and with any luck we'll be picking him up sooner than later. So what's your interest?'

'There you go again Helen always on the defensive. Interested in that case? Not really, just that I heard you lot were doing a good job and I was hoping that passing the case file on helped. I don't think I can win here can I?'

'Ignore me Tony, Sorry I'm just so fucking knackered.'

'It could be another case ticked off the list of many, hey! Be careful though, don't do too good a job Helen you might be permanently assigned to remain over there!'

'You know what Tony, weighing it up, that wouldn't be such a bad thing, you know away from the main building and especially you lot! Left alone to get the job done plus I've got a good bunch of dedicated officers here.'

'Ok, you're busy! I can take a hint! Have a good day, oh, and Helen, don't forget that coffee you've owed me for the past year.'

'Yea sure, I know what your idea of coffee is, speak later.'

*

Saturday morning O6:15 hrs

DI Tony Elms gets on his computer and tracks Smyth's PNC inquiry, tracing North's vehicle registration number. He calls Grant who is going through evidence with DI Guilford.

'Hi it's me, sorry for the early morning call mate, got a pen handy?'

'I'm at the office no probs. Fire away.'

'Private number plate as follows: N1 PTR. Better act quick on this mate. It's red hot.'

'Will do, thanks for the heads-up. Catch up later'.

'Fay, one of my contacts has just supplied me with a vehicle number belonging to North.'

'Ok Paul, let's go.'

Whilst making their way to their vehicle Guilford calls the plate number in. By the time they reach their vehicle North's address details have been patched through to them.

'Let's get ourselves a celebrant, Fay!'

Chapter 22

The previous evening Friday: 27th October.

Helen Smyth is briefing her team on how they are going to arrest Peter North and bring him in for questioning.

'So, one more time, we all meet back here at 07:00 hrs tomorrow, Saturday morning, and then make our way to North's home address. Once there we will pick him up and bring him back here for questioning. My office will be used as the interview room and the interviewees will be myself and Officer Khair.'

'Are we bringing Mr Clifton, the funeral director in too?'

'No Devon, just North, we will see what he has to say for himself first. Quite honestly, I still believe that having met Mr Clifton I think it highly unlikely he's involved. He just doesn't seem the type, this feels more like a one-man-band to me, but you know what though nothing would surprise me.'

Saturday morning 06:50 hrs 28th October

Grant and Guilford arrive at North's home address, Victory House, a five storey building divided into five separate apartments, located in an expensive area of Portsmouth. They make their way up the threshold steps to the front double doors. On the right hand side of the double doors is a panel with five buttons, one for each apartment, with the names of each of the occupants' which are printed in italics and set in small oblong copper edged nameplate.

Guilford scrolls down the panel with her finger, stopping at the third nameplate 'Peter North'. She presses and holds down the button for a few seconds before releasing. They both wait. Guilford presses again, this time holding down the button while she slowly counts up to ten. A tired and weary sounding voice comes from a hidden speaker set in the panel. She releases.

'Hello this is apartment three.....who is it?'

Guilford moves closer to the panel.

'Am I speaking to Mr North?'

'Yes, do you know what bloody time it is?'

'I'm Detective Inspector Fay Guilford from the SCD9 Special Unit and I'm with my colleague DS Paul Grant.'

North yawns. 'You what? I've no idea what the hell you're on about, never heard of you. Christ I've had a late night you know, what is it you want?'

'Sir, it would be best if we spoke face to face.'

'For fuck sake, go on then, show me your ID. Just point it at the camera above you, over to your left.'

Guilford does as North directs.

'Ok, come up. Give me a minute and I'll buzz you in'

A buzzer sounds and the door opens. Inside the foyer there are stairs and a lift. They make the decision to cover both routes. Grant is to make his way up the stairs while Gilford takes the caged elevator. On reaching the 3rd floor, Peter North, is standing outside his door wearing only his boxer shorts, arms akimbo.

'You do realise what time it is don't you?'

'And a good morning to you too Mr North, best we go inside sir.'

'If you must, go on go in.'

Following Grant and Gilford into his apartment North is sure that he has seen Guilford somewhere before.

Once inside Grant and Gilford are taken aback at the space and the luxury of the apartment.

Referring to the cuts and bruises on North's face, Guilford remarks.

'Had a bit of trouble there I see.'

'What, this, oh it's nothing, so, how can I help? North reaches for a pair of jeans hopping from one foot to another as he puts his legs through and pulls them up.

'Mr North, I'm DI Guilford and...'

'Excuse me, but I'm sure I know you from somewhere. What did you say your name was?'

'DI Fay Guilford.'

'Not Fay from the Health Club? Fay! It's me, Peter, the sauna.'

'Peter, no way, I'm sorry I didn't make the connection.'

'You know this guy Fay?'

'Yes Paul purely platonic though, occasionally we bump into each other at the gym.'

Peter this is my colleague DS Paul Grant we are from the SCD9 special unit from the Human Exploitation Organised Crime Command.'

'Human Exploitation, is this some sort of joke?' He reaches for a t-shirt and pulls it on over his muscular body.

DS Grant is annoyed by North's remark, especially having taken an instant dislike to him looking so fit and knowing Fay.

'We're here to take you in for questioning Mr North and believe me, we don't joke.'

'OK, ok. Take me in for questioning? But questioning about what? I know fucking nothing about human exploitation, that's not my scene. You've got to be mistaken.' North reaches down for his socks and shoes, which are beside the settee.

*

From his office window overlooking the police compound, Detective Tony Elms watches DI Smyth and her team climb into their vehicles and drive off. He calls Grant to warn him.

Back at North's apartment Grant gets a call on his mobile. He recognises the name, it's Tony Elms.

'Sorry boss, just stepping out got to take this call.'

'That's ok I'll just wait here until Mr North has finished getting dressed.'

Once outside North's apartment and so as not to be overheard Grant walks down a few steps of the stairwell.

Guilford and North are now on their own 'Ok Fay what's this really all about?'

'Sorry Peter but I can't tell you anything just yet, you'll just have to grin and bear it. If they get the impression that I know you well they would considered the situation compromised then

I might well not be around, taken off the case, especially when you might need my help, so play it down.'

Back outside on the stairwell Grant is talking to Tony Elms.

'Ok mate what have you got?'

'Listen, Smyth and her team, they're on their way, you haven't got long mate.'

'Thanks for the heads up.'

With a real sense of urgency Grant makes his way back to North's apartment.

'Thanks for that Boss, I see he's dressed then, good. Grab your coat Mr North, we'll take your mobile, make safe your apartment, you're coming with us, now!'

North hands his mobile over to Gilford.

'No that's ok officers, I mean about the apartment. He calls out, 'Mia, Mia!'

Mia, the barmaid from The Swan, appears from one of the bedrooms in just her pants and bra.

'Mia I have to pop out. The keys are in the door and there's coffee, cereal and milk, lock up before you leave, catch you later love.'

'Is everything alright Peter?'

'Fine, everything's fine love, don't forget to lock up.'

Mia walks back into the bedroom and closes the door behind her.

'Turn around North, face the wall.'

'Why?'

'Both hands behind your back, now!'

North thinks, this fucker's going to cuff me. 'You've got to be fucking joking.'

'Is there really any need for this Paul.'

'Fay, you know the procedure.'

From a hard leather case attached to his belt Grant pulls out a set of handcuffs and snaps them onto North's wrist, then holding him by his arm leads him out of the apartment followed by Guilford.

Chapter 23

Saturday Morning: 07.00. 28th October.

DI Smyth and the team meet as arranged.

'Ok we have North's address he lives in an apartment called Victories House, The Mews. Officer Baines you're with me, Devon and Khair you will be in the follow up vehicle. We don't all want to turn up at his doorstep and panic him so it will be you and me Baines who will arrest him whilst you Devon and Khair cover the back of the building. Once we have arrested him he's to be taken to my office to be interviewed. Any questions, no? Then ok everyone let's roll.

*

Twenty minutes later DI Smyth and her team arrive at North's address. Officers Khair and Devon make their way to the rear of the building. DI Smyth and Officer Baines stand at the front entrance Smyth presses the intercom, a woman with a hesitant voice answers.

'Hello! Hello can you hear me down there? I don't know if I'm holding the right button down or not. Can you hear me?'

'I can hear you. I'm Detective Inspector Smyth and I have Officer Baines with me. We need to talk to Peter North, please buzz us in so we can come up.'

'Hold on, I've just got to find the right button.'

The door clicks open. They both start to climb the stairs to the third floor, whilst doing so they unwittingly pass Guilford, Grant and Peter North who are on their way down in the lift.

Having knocked on the door of North's apartment, they are left waiting. Mia opens the door wearing a man's dressing gown.

'Mia! I didn't expect it to be you! Baines, this is Mia she works as a barmaid at The Swan. Now, if we can come in.'

Smyth and Baines push their way pass Mia into the main living area.

'Crikey, make yourselves at home will ya I should have guessed you were the Old Bill as soon as I saw you at the Swan. Peter's not here.'

Baines does a quick search of each room.

'He's not here boss.'

'That's what I told you didn't I, he's not here. You don't have much luck when it comes to finding him do ya'

'Go on then Mia, where is he?'

'Well he's obviously not here is he.'

'Ok Mia, cut the bullshit, where is he where has he gone.'

'He's left with some bloke and a woman, what, only a few minutes ago, can't believe you two missed them! I bet you must have passed them on your way up as they went down in the lift, doh! Go on then both of you, run, you and your side kick Robin here might catch them!'

Smyth and Baines quickly make their way out of the apartment and back down the stairs to the foyer. They pass the open doors of the lift and carry on running outside only to see a black SUV pull away at speed, too fast to get its number plate and make.

An exasperated Smyth shouts 'No, no, no, fuck, fuck, fuck!'

Smyth and Baines make their way back up to North's apartment. As they walk in they see Mia tidying the room up.

'Oh no, you two again, bloody Batman and Robin! I take it you lost them then.'

'Do you know who those people were the ones who left with him?'

'No, I was in the bedroom all the time they were here. I did peep through for a look though, didn't recognise them. Look, what's this all about? He's not in trouble is he?'

'Did he say when he or they would be back? Did they say where they were going? Come on Mia! think, what did they say.'

'I could hardly hear what they were saying, anyway I don't like to eavesdrop. Peter did call out to me that he was about to go out and I was to lock up and that he would see me later.'

'When and where later?'

'For Christ sake, I don't know! Later, he could have meant at The Swan, I don't know do I. Look I need to use the loo, I'm bursting, haven't had a pee all night.'

'Are you working today?'

'Unfortunately, yes!'

Baines points to a photograph hanging on the wall. 'Is that North in that photo?'

'Oh he talks then, that officer of yours. It was taken when he was in the armed forces. Still looks the same though, as fit as a fiddle he is.'

'Thanks, we'll be taking that with us.' He takes it down.'

'Peter won't be too pleased you know, it's one of his favourites, mine too. Look I'm sorry but I really have to go before I wet myself.'

'Tough, here's my card, make sure you call me as soon as you see him or if he contacts you.'

'That's it! I'm off before I really do piss my pants. See yourselves out will ya.'

As Mia makes a dash to the toilet Smyth calls out to her.'

'Oh, and Mia, don't forget, I don't want to go arresting you too, so make sure you let me know or I'll have you for perverting the cause of justice.'

'Ok, Ok just make sure you close the fucking door behind you.'

*

Back in the lead vehicle DI Smyth radios through to Officers Devon and Khair, who are still on watch at the rear of the premises.

'Forget it you two, he's gone, stand down and meet us out front in our vehicle.'

Inside Smyth's vehicle they plan their next move. Smyth takes a photo of the picture of North that hung on the wall of his apartment and forwards it to Officers Devon and Khair. Their mobiles ping registering the message as sent.

'I have just sent you a photo of Peter North. It's a few years old but apparently he still looks the same, only without the uniform. I want you Devon and you Khair to keep an watch on The Swan to see if North turns up, it's a good possibility, apart from setting up office there he'll want the keys to his apartment back, the barmaid, has not long got out of his bed and he could be missing her! Baines you stay with me.'

Devon and Khair get into their vehicle and the convoy drives off. As Smyth and Baines make their way back through the Fraud Squad building they are being watched by Detective Tony Elms. He gives a wry smile and makes a call to Grant.

Chapter 24

As Grant and Guilford return with North to the SCD9 Special Unit, Grant gets a call from Tony Elms.

'Got to take this boss, go ahead, I'll catch you up.'

Grant takes the call.

'Hi Tony.'

'Looks like it all turned out well then Paul. I've just seen Helen Smyth walking empty handed through the building and the fucking look on her face mate, it's one of pure thunder.'

'Tony, you saved the day back there mate. It was close, fucking close. As we were pulling away from North's apartment block, I caught a quick glimpse of Smyth and whoever it was she was with standing at the entrance spitting fire. Doubt they had time to get our number. Thank God. I don't know how it happened but it did, Thanks again mate I owe you big time and if you can keep me up to scratch to what she's up to that would be great.'

'No probs Paul catch up soon.'

*

Guilford takes North to an interview room that consist of one table, four chairs, a recording device and in the top left corner of the room a CCTV camera.

'Turn around Peter so I can take those cuffs off you.'

North turns around and faces the wall. Guildford starts to remove the handcuffs.

'Fay, I would never have guessed you were in this line of business.'

He feels relief as his wrists are no longer restricted and shakes his hands to get the blood supply flowing in them again. Guilford lays the handcuffs on the table.

'Ok Peter take a seat.'

'Sure.' He sits down.

'Fay.'

'Yes?'

'I just…' Grant walks into the room.

'Boss before we start can we have a word outside?'

'Yes sure.' They both leave and stand in the corridor.

'What is it Paul?'

'You seem to know this guy pretty well and I'm thinking, should you be sitting in on this interview?'

'Oh come on, I don't know him as such, we've met a few times at our Health Club, well, not even met, met sounds prearranged, more like he was there and I was there, no more than that.'

'Fay look, I just felt I had to air my concern that's all.'

'And I appreciate that. Now let's get in there and do our job.'

Back inside the interview room Guilford and Grant take their seats opposite North.

'Let me introduce myself again Mr North, I'm Detective Inspector Fay Guilford and this is Detective Sergeant Paul Grant. As you know you're not under arrest, you're here to listen to what we have to say.'

'If you say so, I'm all ears.'

'I'm going to open by saying you're a strange one for sure. Peter North the celebrant, Peter North the ex-forces officer with a string of medals and commendations coming out your ears for outstanding services. I don't get it, a celebrant, why, how come? I would have expected someone of your experience to have made the move to protecting Government officials, and the like or at least a job in security or even selling your skills as a mercenary overseas. I don't get it.'

'If you had read my army psychoanalyst's report you would have your answers in front of you. At the end of the day you could say I saw the light.'

Grant intervenes, 'Ok wise guy, listen, you know you're not being charged and you know you're here to hear what we have to say so lighten up. Later it will be time for you to come to a decision on what you're about to hear.'

North thinks, the only wise guy here is you, you fat fuck.'

'So if I'm not being charged and I'm not really interested in whatever the fuck it is you want to tell me, I'm free to go, am I?'

'No. If need be we can think of some trumped up charge to keep you here.'

'No surprise there then, and this thing, is it supposed to mean something to me?'

'Well, it would be in your own best interest to hear us out and then draw your own conclusions.'

Grant intervenes. 'So North, let's start again, we are part of the SDC9 Unit which is a branch of the Human Exploitation Organised Crime Command.'

'So you keep saying, never heard of it and what the hell has it got to do with me anyway?' When you say Human Exploitation you mean people trafficking right? Both women and children.'

'Right and we haven't got the time to be fucked around by the likes of you, do we boss.'

'The likes of me you say. You don't know shit about me you fucking buffoon.'

'Look here you...,

'No DS Grant, no. Peter we have an operation up and running and well, let's say we've hit a problem a major problem and it's just possible you could be of help to us.'

'You couldn't be clearer if you tried, for fuck sake.'

'All you need to know at the moment is that many lives are at risk, you can make the difference between success or failure.'

'Look, Fay, stop there, I've left that kind of heroic crap behind. I keep a low profile these days and I don't want any guilt trip laid on me. So sorry, I can't help, I'm off.'

North stands up. 'I'm out of here, any chance of a lift.'

Grant raises his voice and slams his hands on the table, 'Sit down, shut the fuck up and listen.'

North thinks, wouldn't normally take this crap off of some jerked up shit like you mate, anywhere else and I'd like to see you stop me.

'Get serious Peter it's for real. Look, we both want you to work alongside us, we will guarantee your safety and you would be schooled on what to do and what to say.'

'Safety you say, well Fay, that sounds real ominous and to guarantee my safety! That's a joke if ever there was one. Look you two I've heard that sort of bull-shit countless times during my time in the forces and when push came to shove I'd been left to my own devices to fend for myself. Anyway, why me? I can see how an ex-army man could be useful when it comes to dealing with those bastards who traffic women and children, of course I can and I have a lot of admiration for what you guys do but I've left all that behind and Fay, I'm only interested in my work as a celebrant nowadays.'

'Utilising your work as a celebrant is why we want you,'

'My work as a celebrant, Fay, what the fuck has a celebrant got to do with human exploitation? Are you both nuts?'

'We understand that your role as a celebrant gives you access to families, right.'

'That's right; it's when I find out information about the deceased. You'd be surprised at how many people don't know jack shit about their so-called loved ones. It's not unusual for me to have to pad out what they tell me so it makes the eulogy worth saying and listening to. It gives some credence to the deceased's life. Not to mention the warring family syndrome, well that's what I call it. Some want this and some want that only to be fucking awkward.'

'Look, all we want you to do is your job, only with a little bit of emphasis on certain areas.'

'And doing this helps you to save the lives of those who are being trafficked, how?'

'Look we just need as much information as you can get us on someone who was of interest to us. That someone has recently died and it's his service you will be officiating at.'

'That's uncanny, just goes to show what a small world we live in.'

'You're a comedian as well are you, look North just visit the widow, bring back what you discover and we will piece it all together.'

116

'Hold on mate, if she or the family see through me then I'm basically fucked because this is obviously no way about some ordinary dead guy not by a long-shot. It doesn't take the Brain of Britain to reach that conclusion, associating with you two means that the dead guy must have been heavily involved in human trafficking. That's dangerous territory to be sent into, these trafficking gangs have people everywhere, there would be no hiding places, besides I'd like to hear how you would keep me safe in that situation and by the way how the fuck did you know I was officiating at this guy's funeral service anyway, whoever the fuck he is?'

'DS Grant made some inquiries at J.C. Funeral Service and it so happened they had you down for it.'

'What! James, James Clifton is he part of this charade too? Are you two pulling my shit?'

'Who, who's James Clifton, Paul?'

'Remember boss, He's the one I spoke to, James Clifford the manager at J.C. Funeral Services!'

'Peter, tell me, is James Clifton involved? Is he mixed up in anything else with you, something you would like to share with us? Because you seem to know him well and he would make the perfect front man.'

'Woo hold on there Fay, not sure what you mean there lady, involved, involved in what, not trafficking people, I wouldn't sink that low. If you really think that you're both off your fucking heads?'

'Don't start getting cocky with us North, you know damn well what you've been up to, Boss shall I enlighten him or will you?'

'Tell me what for fuck sake?'

'Leave it to me Paul. Ok, did you know that you are wanted for the crime of fraud? The Cold Case Fraud Unit have you in their sights and ...'

Boss, can I, in actual fact we took you from under their noses minutes before they were about to arrest you at your apartment, did you get that…they were out to arrest you! Why do you think we were in such a rush to get you out? They were coming for you North.'

Guilford thinks, what the fuck is he on about, telling North that Fraud was about to arrest him at his apartment, he couldn't possibly have known that. She recalls Grant stepping outside the apartment to take a call and coming back in a hurried mood. Now if it was the case he knew, who the fuck could have told him?

'I've no idea what the fuck you two are on about, who am I supposed to have defrauded?'

'Oh, come off it North, save it for Fraud. DI Guilford's telling you how it is, so let's drop all the bull shit and get real. The question you should be asking yourself is, am I fucked, and the answer to that is a big fat yes. You are fucked. It comes down to this, you either work for us or we hand you over to Fraud.'

North is taken aback at first then he thinks, you fuckers think you have me over a barrel here, but you're dealing with a different animal here, I have my ways. It looks to me as if you need me more than you are letting on. Play the fuckers.

'So, let me see if I've got this right, you two want me to risk my life and Fraud want to see me banged up behind bars. Give me a second to think about that, it's a no brainer, call Fraud.'

'Come on, he doesn't mean that boss, you don't mean that do you North, not with your military experience. You're obviously used to being in the danger zone and don't tell me you don't miss the buzz, guys like you thrive on it.'

'I get all the buzz I need doing what I do.'

'Bull shit North, think on, that will be short lived if Fraud get their hands on you. Look, do this for us and for all those who are caught up in trafficking and it will go a long way in helping your case. Yes of course Fraud will eventually press for criminal charges but, hey, nowhere near as severe as they could be if you assist us. We have already checked your background and know that since the Forces you have picked up a few criminal convictions on the way so will we find you're breaking the law working as a celebrant, more than likely. Surely no one does that job if they have a criminal record?'

'Fay, tell your baboon that celebrants aren't checked for their criminal records, that's why I took the job on in the first place.'

'We'll look into it Peter.'

Grant interrupts. 'So what's it to be? Stop pulling my dick, yes or no? We haven't got the time to be pissed about, have we boss?'

'No, we have a deadline to meet, lives are at risk and it's coming at us fast. Are you in or do I make the call to the Cold Case Fraud unit to come and get you?'

'You should have explained all this in the beginning you two, but no you both had to play your fucking little games. I'll do it, but any shit from you in particular dick head,' he points at Grant. 'And I'm out.'

'No one else knows about this you understand? Not even the lovely Mr Clifton. As far as he or anyone else is concerned you're doing what you have done on many previous occasions as a celebrant. Right Paul we need to get the ball rolling. The name of the deceased is a Mr Dennis Forrester and the funeral service is arranged for November 15th.'

North thinks, this is crazy, are these guys are talking about Lisa's old man? No way, no it couldn't be. If it is, what the fuck has he been up to deserve the attention of this lot, and most importantly does Lisa have any idea.

'Have you been in contact with the family yet in regard to arranging a home visit?'

'Dennis Forrester you say, well I'm pretty sure that a service is booked in for that date, but under what name I haven't been told yet. I'm waiting for J.C. to get back to me on that. It's what, just over two weeks away from now, a bit too early to make contact with the family. Things will still be a bit raw, you know, upsetting, so to answer your question no, I haven't.'

'Then you need to arrange a visit, you can do that now while you're here and, as soon as you can, a follow up visit a day or two later.'

'Ok that shouldn't be a problem but the contact number is on my mobile, sent to me in a confirmation email, so I'm going to need it back.'

Grant opens the door of the interview room and calls along the corridor for assistance, a uniformed guard approaches him. Grant asks for North's belongings to be brought to the interview room ASAP, he waits at the door. Soon after, the guard returns and hands over North's belongings which had been stored in an evidence bag. Grant steps back into the interview room, opens the evidence bag and tips the mobile phone on to the table, picks it up and hands it to North.

'Here, make the call.'

While waiting for the mobile to find a signal, North, hopes that Guilford and Grant are not going to be listening in to the call.

Guilford and Grant watch and wait as North scrolls through his emails locating the confirmation email sent from J.C. Funerals.

'Ah, got it.'

He tries to give Guilford and Grant the impression that he is mentally noting the number, but then, unknown to them, he already knows it.

He dials the number, a youngish voice answers.

'Can I help you?'

'Hello, my name is Peter North and I have been given your number by J.C. Funeral Services in regard to Mr Dennis Forrester's funeral service, May I speak with Mrs Forrester please.'

'Hold on, I'll go and get her.'

To make it impossible for Guilford and Grant to overhear the conversation he presses the mobile phone firmly against his ear and stealthily edges the volume down.

'Hello.'

'Am I speaking to Mrs Forrester?'

'Of course, you know it's me Peter, stop messing.'

North turns his back on Guilford and Grant.

'Mrs Forrester, may I first start by offering you my sincere condolences over the loss of your husband Dennis. My name is Peter North and I am a celebrant. I have been given your number by J.C. Funeral Services in regard to arranging your husband's Funeral Service.'

'Oh, oh yes, thank you, yes, the Funeral Director said that you would be in contact with me,' She whispers. 'Hi, darling, you sound so formal, quite sexy; I take it you can't talk freely.'

North manages to keep his composure as Guilford and Grant look on. He gives them the thumbs up sign

'That's correct Mrs Forrester. To enable Dennis's service to be as you would like, I was hoping to arrange a visit with you so we can talk it through, possibly for tomorrow.'

This time, North gets the thumbs up from Guilford, and Grant shows his full agreement with a nod.

'Tomorrow you say Mr North?'

'Yes, only if that is convenient for you of course.'

'I'm out in the morning so can we make it say, 12:30?' She whispers. 'I miss you Peter.' He thinks 'Just shut the fuck up.'

He looks at Guilford and Grant, there is no reaction. He presses the mobile harder to his ear.

'12:30 will be fine Mrs Forrester.'

'Oh, do you want the address and post code of Mortimer House. Mr North?'

'Thank you but I already have it, courtesy of J.C. Funeral Services.'

'Well darling you know the routine. Stop at the main gate, security will meet you and accompany you to the house. Expect you tomorrow.' She hangs up.

'Looks like I'm on for tomorrow, 12.30. Now what do you two want me to do Fay?'

'Write down the questions you would normally ask during a visit, we will read through them and incorporate some of ours without it becoming too obvious. Oh and you might be wearing a wire so we can monitor the situation. And by the way, we have made a bed up for you in one of our cells, you'll be staying here tonight.'

North recalls the nights he has spent in a cell, he thinks, I can live with that.

'What the fuck do you hope to achieve by keeping me here overnight?'

'It helps us keep a tight lid on events North. We wouldn't want him being picked-up by the other lot now, would we boss?'

'No. Peter, we will be taking your mobile back and don't worry, you won't be locked in. Okay let's all take a break and get something to eat I don't know about you two but I'm starving.'

Chapter 25

Chief Inspector Edinburgh makes a phone call to Chief Inspector Munro of Fraud.

'Chief Inspector Edinburgh here from the SCD9 Special Unit, I want to inform you that my people have picked up a chap who we believe may have been on your radar. If that is the case I do apologise, it was far from intentional I can assure you. What we require from this chap has no bearing on and nor is it related to fraud and of course, as soon as my people have finished with him we will hand him over to you.'

'Well Detective Chief Inspector Edinburgh, I know nothing of this as of yet but I can assure you that the unit involved is going to be spitting nails over this. However what's done is done. Who is this person and how did you get to hear about him?'

'Now let me see, yes, his name is Peter North he's been connected to a premises we have marked down as being 'highly significant' to an ongoing investigation of ours.'

'So, how did you know this North character was known to us?'

'Our surveillance noted one of your DI's along with an Officer entering and leaving the said premises, they put two and two together and concluded that Peter North may have been sort after by your DI. Now, I apologise once more if this was the case and will keep you up to scratch, thank you.'

'Thank you for letting me know.'

As Munro replaces the receiver, DI Smyth knocks and walks in.

'Just keeping you in the loop sir, the file you sent me had some excellent results. It means that we have a suspect and his name is Peter North who may relate to quite a few cold cases and...'

'Stop there Helen, I have just had a call from Chief Inspector Edinburgh from the SCD9 Special Unit, they have North in their custody.'

'Excuse me! SCD9 have Peter North!'

'That's correct.'

'Isn't SCD9 a Human Trafficking Unit?'

'It is yes.'

'Now what the hell are they doing with him, he's a celebrant for Christ sake not someone who traffics people.'

'No mention I'm afraid, just that they have him and they will hand him over to us when they have done with him. So, what's this Peter North to us?'

'North's our main suspect connected to a backlog of cases and a recent case. Sir I don't believe this, I really don't. It must have been them who beat us to arresting him and it's not just a coincidence they did. Sir, I mean how did that happen? You know what, something's not right here. Ok, let me think,' She paces about the office. 'So they can't be charging him with anything or they wouldn't be willing to hand him over to us. But what's a celebrant got to do with trafficking people. I mean it's crazy. Could be they knew we were on to North before they grabbed him, you know, let him know we were going to arrest him and use that as leverage to make some sort of deal? And why, what's to make a deal over. I just don't get it.'

'That could well be the case and maybe we will never know but he's there for a reason and reasons that are only known to them.'

'So what do they suppose I do? Sit on my ass and be grateful for their generosity, Christ. OK we still have a number of cold cases to follow up, so when North is finally in our custody, I'll make damn sure that the case against him is iron clad,'

'Hear me out Helen, you are not to interfere in any way, shape or form with SCD9's investigation, the last thing I want is top brass bloody well breathing down my neck.'

'But Sir I ....'

'Helen, no buts, I know what you're like. They will be in contact! Now, close the door on the way out.'

'Yes Sir'

She thinks, no way am I going to wait for North to be handed over, no way.'

Chapter 26

Its mid-morning and John Mayfair sits in his car which is parked a few cars down from the front entrance of the apartment block where North lives. Today is payment day. Mayfair pours himself coffee from a flask, slightly opening his side window to help stop the windscreen from misting up. He calls Joan Maxwell.

'Mrs Maxwell.'

It takes a few seconds for her to recognise his voice. She speaks in a drunken slur.

'Mayfair...I take it you have some good news for me?'

'Yes, I've met with North and everything is in hand.'

'Good, just fucking make sure you get it back, all of it.'

'I will, you can be assured of that. Oh, Mrs Maxwell I...' She hangs up, he thinks, fuck you too, you piss head.

He makes a call to North, it goes to voicemail. *'You have reached the voicemail of Celebrant Peter North, leave a message and I will be sure to return your call as soon as I am available. Thank you.'* A short silence is followed by a beep.

Having disconnected the call Mayfair finishes his coffee then pulls a pillow from the back seat and puts it between his head and the headrest, putting on a set of headphones and half reclining his seat he settles back, listening to *'Lover'* by Taylor Swift and waits for however long it takes for North to return.

*

There is a knock on the cell door. North is already awake. Guilford walks in carrying breakfast consisting of two slices of toast accompanied by a mug of coffee on a tray. A multi-coloured toiletry bag hangs over her left shoulder. She places both the tray and bag, on the floor of the cell as North who is laying on the bed, bare-chested, props himself up against one of the smooth but cold, white washed brick walls of the cell.

126

Guilford is more than pleasantly surprised to see North's athletic frame again.

'What time is it Fay? My watch is over there in the corner on top of my clothes, have a look will you?'

She declines the offer and looks at her watch instead.

'It's 7am, I've brought you breakfast and inside the toiletry bag, which, by the way is mine so take care of it, you'll find toothpaste, a new toothbrush, soap, gear to shave with. I presume you wet shave, if not tough, you'll even find a comb in there as well. I've arranged for an officer to bring you a towel shortly. So, sort yourself out and one of my officers will collect you in about 45 mins. Oh, and you're lucky, there's hot running water today.'

'Thanks Fay and it's a good morning to you too! No chance of a shower then!'

With the thought of that in mind she smiles and walks out of the cell. Before pulling the cell door partly closed behind her she changes her mind and walks back in.

'You know Peter I was really hoping that we would sort of, you know, get some kind of a relationship going. I mean, our chats at the sauna meant a lot to me. It wasn't coincidence I happened to be there, I arranged my time so it would coincide with you being there. I'd see you working-out and I thought I'd like to know you better. The sauna was the place to talk to you, get you on your own, you know, to get to know you. Christ I really wanted that.'

'Fay,' His left hand pats the bed. 'Come and sit here, you're safe I don't bite.'

North shuffles closer to the wall making room for her to sit on the side of the narrow bed.

Guilford closes the cell door and sits on the side of the bed facing him.

'Peter I…'

'Fay,' North chances it by gently touching her fingertips with his, she doesn't pull away. 'I know exactly what you mean, I was hoping for the same. I guess it wouldn't have been long before we inevitably got it together, it was the next stage. Talking of the sauna Fay, I just loved the way those beads of sweat contoured you curves, baby it got me hotter than the actual heat coming from the steam! It really set the day up for me.'

Guilford smiles as she moves her hand along one of his bare muscular arms.

'I know what you mean. Why you Peter? Why couldn't it have been another Peter North that's sitting in this cell?'

He thinks, she really has got the hots for me. 'Yeah, I know what you fucking mean but all is not lost, I'll beat this, but I think I'm going to need your help,' he leans forward and kisses her, he feels her respond as her lips press into his. 'Can I rely on you Fay, can I?'

'Yes you can.... You know I'd better be out of here, the officer bringing you the towels will be here at any moment. Listen, you will be allowed to go back to your apartment after we have spoken to you, I'll see you back there.'

'Look forward to it.'

'Christ, I am to.'

Before standing up from the bed, Guilford and North share some deep tongue kissing. She pulls away.

'Got to go, enjoy you breakfast, although it's probably stone cold now!'

'I've had worse.'

Chapter 27

North is eventually collected from his cell by a uniformed officer and taken to the same interview room as before.

Memories flood his mind, back to a time when he was being escorted in double time by five Red Caps, taken from the army slammer to the courthouse. Being in the centre of the tight knit group of men the short march was intense. It seemed faster than a traditional double-time, more like verging on an all-out run and the constant bellowing of left right, left right, left right, left right, left right from one of the Red Caps only added to the pressure. As he was being hurriedly shepherded along North was forced to keep close to the nape of the neck of the shaven headed Red Cap in front of him. Clipping his heals and tripping was not an option. With the shout of halt and the slamming down of army boots they came to a halt and following more bellowing orders the five Red Caps marched off leaving North standing in front of a panel of Officers. North stood to attention and saluted before being given the order to stand at ease.

*

North is left waiting for Guilford and Grant to show up. As he paces about the room he stops occasionally to do a few Taoist breathing and stretching exercises which he learnt during his spare time when he was stationed in the Far East. It eventually takes around twenty minutes for Gilford and Grant to show up.

'Good morning Peter! Take a seat.'

A uniformed officer follows them in carrying three fresh cups of coffee on a tray. Taking the cups from the tray he places them onto the table and leaves. Grant slides one over to North, the other to Guilford.

'Ok North, we have gone over examples of your notes looking at the generic questions you would ask. It all reads well but we just need you to dig deeper, broaden out your questioning more so than you normally would. DI Guilford.'

'That's right we want you to find out as much as you can about Dennis Forrester's life and his activities. When writing down your notes, under the subtitle 'Family and Friends' press it a bit more when she's telling you about associates and their names. Over the years she could possibly have been introduced to some of them or better still know something about them. If you think she's wondering why you're asking explain like you would do, it's so you can add the people to the welcoming part of the service and to also include them in the eulogy you're going to be writing up, DS Grant.'

'Yes boss, try and find out if there will be associates travelling from abroad to attend the funeral service, if so, again, who are they and where are they travelling from? When asking about holidays, do as you normally would and find out when and where they've been. Whatever country she mentions tell her it's always been a place you've wanted to visit, so get her to elaborate, can she describe or recommend any landmarks and what places did they visit whilst they were there, boss.'

'Also, who was it she and her husband stayed with when they were at any of these places and most importantly will any of them be attending the funeral service? If so who? DS Grant.'

'In a nutshell North, get every bit of info you can about Dennis Forrester's life.'

'For fucks sake, some double act you two are. Have you rehearsed this or what! Look no worries I've got it covered.'

'Fair enough, you supply that info and we'll do the rest.'

'Like I said, I've got it covered. Remember though, I help you, you help me. So, I'm free to go now am I? Mia will still have the keys to my apartment.' He looks at his watch. 'Better for me if you drop me off at The Swan, I'll get a taxi from there, she'll be doing a bit of early morning cleaning.'

'Fine, collect your keys, you won't need a taxi we'll drop you back at your apartment where you can get a change of clothes, plus whatever you need for the visit. Remember you will be under surveillance at all times. DI Guilford.'

'Don't forget, after visiting Mrs Forrester, drive straight back to your apartment and wait for our call. We will bring you back here for a debrief. Have you got that? Come on, I need convincing, convince me Peter, convince us both.'

'Look, how many times for fuck sake! I've got it covered. There's too much riding on this for all concerned for me to fuck it up.'

Chapter 28

Mayfair has seen many vehicles come and go from his vantage point but his attention is soon drawn to a black SUV that pulls up at speed. He sees North jump out and make his way hurriedly up the threshold steps leading to the apartment block entrance. The black SUV speeds away.

Mayfair mutters to himself, 'Now where have you been Mr North, hopefully getting my money. And there was me making the mistake of thinking you were in your apartment because your car was outside, an amateur's mistake on my part Mr North.'

*

Once inside his apartment North undresses. Anxious to rid himself of the clinging odour of the police cell he jumps under the shower. With his head under the fast flowing showerhead he can't hear his mobile phone ringing. It's not until he bends down to soap his legs with top of the range shower gel the ringing coming from the phone cuts through. He rinses his legs down, grabs a towel, rushes into the living room, throws the towel onto the carpet and stands bare-assed on it, grabs hold of the phone and answers.

'Hello.'

'It's Fay. I'm parked at the back of the building, can I get in from here, SCD9 surveillance has the front covered?'

'Fay! Yes of course, wow I mean yes. You should be able to see a door to the left of the building and the code for the security lock is c7773x.'

'I can see it, c7773x you say, I'm on my way.' North thinks, fuck, she really does have the hots for me and that can only be to my favour.

Guilford makes her way to the door and punches in the code. Turning the small metallic handle she pushes the door open and

132

steps inside. She makes her way up a short flight of stairs and stops, the loud sound of the lift's pulleys and mechanisms kicking into action as the lift rises up to one of the floors, makes her jump. She can hear the lift's doors sliding open and decides to takes the stairs. She taps on the door of North's apartment. Wearing only a bath towel wrapped around his waist he lets her in. No sooner has she taken her coat off she pushes North up against a wall and starts to madly kiss him, he frantically undoes the buttons on her blouses slides it off her shoulders and lets it fall to the floor, As she presses her breast into his chest, North reaches behind her to unclip the clasp on her bra, she steps back allowing North to pull it over her arms and discard it. She presses herself into him harder and holds his arms outstretched, as in the shape of a crucifixion. 'Stay like that.' she says breathing heavily. She lowers herself down on to her knees and loosens the towel from North's waist it drops to the floor. She takes hold of his semi hard penis in one hand the other grips hold of one of his tight buttocks. As she slowly runs her soft lips and hot breath along his penis she feels it harden as blood pumps through its veins. She then deep throats him, North looks down amazed at how far she could take it down her throat. He reaches down and grabs her breasts. Now, both hands holding on his buttocks, she sucks fast and furious. North pulls away, he doesn't want to ejaculate just yet, he wants to finish off but inside her, He stands her up, turns her around and positions her hands flat against the wall then lifts her dress up over her ass, parts her wet pants to one side and pushes his hard penis inside her. Every one of his thrust makes her scream with ecstasy. She feels North is about to cum, feeling his penis penetrating deeper and harder with every quickening thrust. She tightens her virginal muscles as he explodes inside her, she climaxes out of her skull.

Chapter 29

According to his watch, Mayfair mentally logs that it has been an hour and thirty-five minutes since North went into the apartment block, another ten minutes goes by before he appears outside and hurriedly gets into his car then drives away. Mayfair decides not to follow. He doesn't want to risk compromising any situation in which North may be raising the money.

Mayfair pours himself another coffee, turns up the volume on his headphones and lies back listening to The Rolling Stones album, '*Beggars Banquet*' and as he does so he starts to think about what led him up to this point in his life.

As a young boy Mayfair remembers how difficult he found it adjusting to living in Tottenham North London having just moved with his parents from the Gambia and was regularly mistaken by his teachers, school friends and later in life as a teenager, as being from the West Indies. He recalls being victimised and scared, made to feel like an outsider, especially by the threats that came from the English gangs of the time. How he thought it wise and for his own protection, to promote himself as being from the West Indies and joined a Jamaican gang which was solely made up of young Jamaicans'. He remembers how he had to pass the initiation test set for him by Prosper, the gang leader, before being accepted as a full-time member. And should he think about ripping the gang off, Prosper stressed that he knew where his family lived. Mayfair was given instructions to make his way to Shepherds Bush station on a Saturday afternoon arriving at 2pm where someone going by the name of Jim would be waiting on the platform to make the transaction, money for dope. North was to hand over a rucksack containing two 1.lb weights of Moroccan black and in return he would receive £300, and obviously hand it over to Prosper on his return to Tottenham.

Mayfair remembers how his journey was far from an ordinary one. It began by catching a number 259 bus from Tottenham to Manor House underground train station. He then travelled on the Piccadilly Line before picking up the Central Line at Kings Cross. Travelling on the underground on Saturday at that time of day meant that the carriages were going to be jam packed full of noisy, loud chanting, football fans who were on their way to the Arsenal football ground for the local derby between Arsenal and Tottenham Hotspur. Memories of that part of the journey made Mayfair laugh to himself. Three police officers, one with a police dog had entered the carriage of the train, two stations before Arsenal, in the hope that their presence and the barking police dog would avoid day to day passengers being harassed by supporters and any destruction to the carriages. Mayfair had thought, fucking hell I don't believe it, as he found himself along with his backpack which contained the dope, squashed in between the police officers and police dog which was on a short choker chain, tongue hanging out and panting heavily and kept whining, nudging its handler's hand as if to get his attention. The police dog made two attempts, in the tight space it had, to jump up at Mayfair. He thought, for fuck sake please don't let that be one of those sniffer dogs. The dog handler jerked the choker lead back and told the police dog to sit, it did, but continued to sniff at Mayfair's legs and groin. The doors of the train slid shut, it felt stifling, claustrophobic and as it pulled out of the station all those standing lurched in the opposite direction then back again before constantly swaying from side to side as the noisy train travelled along its uneven tracks underground. One of the police officers looked down and saw Mayfair looking up at him.

'Alright son, Alfie here won't bite you, and stop looking so worried there will be no trouble here.'

'Yes officer, I mean no officer.'

'Off to the match are you?'

'No, I'm meeting a friend of mine in Shepherds Bush.'

The song 'You'll Never Walk Alone' erupted from the football supporters.

The police office had to shout so Mayfair could hear him. 'Well, you stay beside us son and we'll make sure you're kept safe from this lot.'

Mayfair shouted back 'Thank you.'

The police dog strained at the choke lead in its vain attempt to jump up at him again. The dog handler jerked at the lead back and the police dog retreated.

'You can tell your friend that you've had a police escort today son.'

'Thank you officer I will. They'll never believe it!'

*

It wasn't long before the train reached Kings Cross station, the police, police dog and the football fans had already disembarked at Arsenal, some stations before.

He remembers making his way through the tunnel like corridors of Kings Cross underground tube station and how he struggled when trying to make sense of the large map of the underground network. Having found his way to the Central Line further examination of the underground network caused him to panic when he realised that the station he wanted, Shepherds Bush, was in fact two different stations, one above ground as well as one underground, Shepherd's Bush Market and Shepherd's Bush Central he plumped for the station above ground, Shepherd's Bush Market.

He arrived at Shepherds Bush Market at 1.50 pm. He sat on one of the platforms benches and waited, as he was told to. It was now getting on for 2.20, several trains had arrived and left during that time leaving the platform deserted, no one called Jim approached him. He got to thinking he had made a massive mistake and should have gone to Shepherds Bush Central instead and that he had blown any chance of becoming a member of Prosper's Jamaican gang.

On the opposite platform, he noticed two men slowly pacing to and fro, occasionally stopping to look across at him. He watched them as they made their way across the bridge that joined the North and South bound platforms and walked towards him. One of them wore a small round framed pair of dark sunglasses and was wearing a bright red and white polka dot waistcoat buttoned over a fat stomach that bulged from under an unbuttoned long heavy coat with every step he took his cane scraped along the platform. It became obvious to Mayfair that the man was blind and reliant on the other man, who was tall and thin, to lead the way and to keep trackside of him. They came to a halt at the bench. Mayfair stood up and was sure that the blind man could see him behind his dark lenses. The tall thin man spoke.

'Are you John?'

Suspicious, Mayfair walked away and stopped at the bottom of the steps to the bridge. The thin man caught him up leaving the blind man sitting on the bench.

'You're John, right.'

'That's right.'

'Prospect sent you, right.'

'That's right.'

'Ok, as you leave the station you'll see opposite that there are some big factory wooden gates, they'll be open. See you there in ten minutes. I'll just go get my friend.'

He remembers how he ran as fast as he could up the steps that led him across the bridge and down the other side, he handed his ticket over to a ticket collector and made his way outside. He bent over forwards with his hands on his knees as he tried to catch his breath. In front of him, across the road, were the big open wooden gates. It wasn't long before the two men came out of the station and crossed the road to where he was standing.

'Have you got it?'

'Yes, have you got the money?'

'What do you think, now where is it?'

'Look, I've got it ok. I need you to hand me the money and I'll hand the shit over. I'm too scared to rip you and Prosper off, that's not going to happen, trust me but at the same time I don't want to get ripped off too, Prosper's expecting to be paid.'

The tall man holds out a large brown envelope. 'Here, take it.'

North remembers how he nervously opened the envelope and saw a bundle of notes of various denominations. That was good enough for him.

'The dope now young man if you please.'

'It's there,' he points to one of the big gates. 'Behind that gate, it's inside the rucksack.'

He had no sooner said that when he ran away along the road and for the first time in his life he hailed a taxi. No matter the cost, he wanted out of there even if it meant sacrificing his rucksack.

Chapter 30

Making his way to the pre-arranged visit at Mortimer House, North re-connects the car's audio system to the Bluetooth app on his mobile and makes a call to Lisa Forrester.

'Hi Lisa it's me Peter, sorry about earlier. Lisa, I had no idea that your husband Dennis had passed away. You didn't mention it to me, I thought that y...'

'Peter, I was going to, I mean, I meant to of course I was, I, I, just wasn't thinking straight, sorry.'

'No probs, you've got nothing to be sorry about, but I must say it did come as a bit of a surprise.'

'So, tell me how did you find out that Denis had died?'

'Funeral director James Clifton had me down to officiate at a Mr Forrester's funeral service, I didn't make the connection until yesterday and yet it's not an uncommon name.'

'My God, I didn't even make the connection myself, you know, the fact that you might work for this Clifton guy, sorry, now I feel so foolish. The call you made to me yesterday, I guessed you had someone with you hence the formality?'

'Yeah, thanks for playing along with me back there, I'll explain when I see you, I'm on my way to yours now.'

'I'll be waiting.'

After disconnecting the call, North thinks, fucking strange, her not telling me that her old man's dead, am I missing something here, for that is what I call fucking weird!

One month earlier:

Two days after Donald James Maxwell's funeral service, North is in The Swan working on the eulogy for his next service when he receives a call, it's an unknown number.

'Hi is that Peter North the celebrant?'

'Speaking how can I help?'

'This is Lisa Forrester, we met a few days ago. I'm the mad woman who ran up to you in the pouring rain, whilst being consumed by an umbrella, at the crematorium. Remember? I asked you for a business card!'

'Not exactly, no.'

'Look, you had been doing that talking stuff at my friend Joan Maxwell's husband's funeral service, Donald Maxwell.'

Having realised that this is one of the three women who fucked about during Maxwell's funeral service, he wasn't going to make this easy for her. 'Forrester you say, Lisa Forrester, nope, doesn't ring any bells. Do you require my professional services or do I report this as a scam call?'

'No. well yes, no I mean I…'

'Listen, I'm only winding you up! I remember you, of course I do, I mean, how could I possibly forget, I've still got the scars from your umbrella kept poking me in the head!'

'Peter North, you are beginning to make me feel very stupid!'

'Apologies,' this woman has no sense of humour, that's for sure, 'So, how are you?'

'I'm good thanks! You know what's so sweet?'

'What?'

'You, having remembered me of course.'

'I've been called many things in my life but sweet, never! We didn't get off on the best footing did we?'

'I was hoping we could put that behind us.'

'You can try.'

140

'Ok, you know I was really impressed by how you handled the service, it's something I could never do, you know, stand in front of all those people. How do you do it? I couldn't help thinking as I sat there, just how good looking you ..... Oops! Sorry, that just slipped out.'

'Right-e oh,' He is reminded of his school days when in the playground girls would hang around him and tease him because of his good looks and because of this he didn't have many friends to play with, boys that age didn't have time for the opposite sex, but a young Peter North did and always would.

'Ok Peter, this is going to sound a bit forward of me, well a lot actually, and by the way, you're not making this easy for me, you know that don't you.' North thinks, just spit it out will you for fuck sake. 'Can we meet up for a drink?'

'Meet up you say, for a drink, well, I would have to think long and hard about that, you know the sort of thing, would it be unethical of me taking in account my line of work.'

'Oh I didn't mean to... '

'Ha! That's twice I've got you! Sure, that would be real nice. Just say when and where.'

'Will you pack it in, I mean the fooling around,' she pauses to think. 'Well not where I live that's for sure! I was thinking possibly 'The Barons Hotel' do you know where it is?'

'No, but I'll find it, there can't be many places that go by that name. Oh, one more thing, remind me, Lisa isn't it, your name I mean?'

'Lisa, Lisa Forrester. Look Peter, I'm really beginning to go off you!'

'Ok, no more messing I promise. I'm actually free this evening!'

'I am too!'

'7pm?'

'7pm it is.'

*

North arrives at The Barons Hotel, an ancient building converted to a hotel in Edwardian times, at exactly 6.55pm and makes his way inside to the bar where he pulls up a stool. He is

141

approached by one of the bar staff and asked if he is ready to order. He explains that he is expecting company and wants to wait a while. In the reflection of one of the big mirrors that hang behind the bar emphasising the different sizes and shapes of bottles and their varied coloured contents he see Lisa Forrester approaching from behind. She places both hands on his shoulders. He holds his hands up in the air.

'Ok, I surrender!'

Lisa laughs. 'Peter, Hi.'

He swivels around on his stool and faces her.

'Hi Lisa, saved you one, take a seat. You look different, a good different though.'

'Thanks, different hair style, bearing in mind I was trying to keep on a fascinator you know a hat, the last time you saw me, an impossible task in the wind and rain but yes, a different hair style.'

North tries unsuccessfully to get the attention of the bar-staff he had only just minutes ago sent away. Lisa soon starts to feel uncomfortable as there are too many people in the vicinity for her liking. She is too much on show and in the company of a man.

'Peter let's find a more private seating area, I can see just the place.'

North follows her and as he does so he can't take his eyes off of the movement of her shapely backside. North is led to an empty booth, its semi-curved leather seating copying the curve of the smoked-glass table. They find themselves sitting at opposite ends so they each shuffle along the seat until they meet in the middle, positioning themselves slightly sideways on to face each other.

A waitress approaches and lights the candle that is positioned in the middle of the table then asks their drinks order. Forrester orders a bottle of Krug Grande Cuv'ee Brut and North orders Whiskey on the Rocks.

'Peter thank you so much for coming, it's a lovely place don't you agree.'

'It's ok.'

'It's more than just ok! There's history attached to this building that goes way back before Edwardian times, for example did you know that The Baron is a British Hereditary Dignitary, first created by King James I of England, a long time ago, in May 1611? Not only that, the baronetage is not, as some might think, part of the peerage, nor is it an order of knighthood.'

'I must admit Lisa, I haven't given it much thought but this place does, in a way, reflect that vibe, it still manages to capture a feel, a sense, an ambiance of its historic value. The architects that oversaw the conversion over the years have shown great sympathy to the original build.'

She starts to laugh, 'Oh Peter you are so funny!'

'What do you mean? Why are you laughing?'

'You, trying to impress me, I know nothing about the history of this place I was only reciting from that plaque hanging over the bar, getting my own back, winding you up like you did twice to me when I called you earlier!'

North looks across and up at the plaque and smiles.

'Ok you got me there big time! You know I even impressed myself!'

Two waiters approach, one holding an ice bucket containing the bottle of champagne and a small white towel draped over his arm, the other carrying the whisky and a champagne glass on a tray. The waiter places the ice bucket on the table, removes the bottle of champagne, wipes it with the towel, then with no theatricals removes its cork and pours a small amount into the champagne glass slightly angled.

'Madam, if you will.' Lisa takes a sip of the champagne.

'Yes, that will do nicely, thank you.' The waiter adds more champagne to the glass then places it down.

'Thank you Madam.'

The waiter then, as if well-choreographed, steps back to allow the other one to step forward with North's whiskey, he places it on a table mat then both waiters return to the bar.

Left on their own Lisa stares at North

'What!'

'I can look can't I?'

'I guess you can.'

'Peter this meeting is strictly between us you understand, if my friend Zara, that's Zara Maxwell, found out that I was sat here having a drink with the man who was hired to oversee her husband's funeral service, she would kill me.'

'No worries. So, tell me something about yourself.'

'Like my friend Zara Maxwell, my husband and I are extremely well off and I guess it's that age old story of woman feeling ignored by busy husband, so woman finds a lover, well you know the rest.'

'Too busy for you, he must be mad! What sort of work is it that takes him away from you?'

'I'm afraid that's one question I won't be answering. Put it this way, I'm a woman who enjoys pure luxury and lots of attention, he keeps me in the manner I deserve to be kept in but there are times though when I find that that's not enough.'

'And that's where I come in right?'

'Yes, that's where you come in. Why, you make it sound as if it's going to be such hardship. I'm beautiful don't you know and that makes you a very, very lucky man! So, let's make a toast, to you and me.'

They raise their glasses.

'To us.'

'I'll drink to that Lisa, to us.'

Chapter 31

On his arrival at Mortimer House, North comes to a halt at the main gate, he winds the side window down as the security guard walks over to him and looks into the car.

'Good to see you again Mr North welcome to Mortimer House.' As he scrolls down his mobile app he stops: *it reads: Peter North appointment 1pm.* 'OK Mr North, drive on, you will find parking places to the right of the main entrance today. Have a good day sir.'

'Thank you.'

Having parked up, North makes his way to the entrance of the house. Shortly after ringing the doorbell he is invited to step inside by the housekeeper and shown to a large room. He looks at the thick lush carpet with a smile, having made love to Lisa on it last time he was here. The room is dominated by the three impressive large settees: a Westminster Button three seater sofa, a Bakerfield 3 Seater leather sofa and a Carolina 2 Seater Loveseat Marlow all facing towards the large ornate open fireplace. The housekeeper leaves the room closing the door behind her.

At first glance, North can't see Lisa as she sits hidden behind the tall back of the Carolina 2 Seater. She comes into view as she stands up and walks towards North. They both embrace and kiss each other passionately.

'Peter I've missed you like crazy.'

'Lisa we must talk, there have been developments, things that involve us both. It's not about our affair, no-one knows about that so you're safe there, but other crazy things are starting to happen.'

'Actually Peter, right now, I don't give a shit who knows about us, not now that Dennis has gone. What's he going to do, haunt me! Anyway, what things are you talking about?'

They sit down on the Westminster Button three seater sofa.

'Lisa, can you remember when we first met I asked you what your husband did for a living. You said you were not prepared to answer. I was more than happy to leave it at that, let it go, but now that Dennis is no longer with us do you think you can you share with me what he did.'

'I'm not sure I can Peter but at the same time I don't want there to be any secrets between us and it does seem important to you. Dennis was not a nine to five man, far from it, no, he wasn't that type. The money, well, I must admit he made a great deal of it. All through our engagement and since the day we married he remained cagey about what he did and where the money came from. I would play host to his friends and associates and that seemed to be my main role in life. The men, well they would often retreat to what was referred to as the 'knowledge room' to discuss business. In the summer they would often sit around the pool smoking large cigars and drinking. Of course it crossed my mind, and I had suspicions, whether or not what Dennis did was illegal, I guess I kept away from wanting to know the truth. It was all good. So, why now why do you want to know about Dennis? You're beginning to worry me, please tell me what the hell this is all about?'

'Okay, so you weren't aware that Dennis was someone of importance to the police or even may have been under police surveillance?'

'No, how could I? You're not making this any clearer you know'

'Yesterday two Detectives came to my apartment and took me in for questioning.'

'Oh my God! What for, what did they want? Had it something to do with Dennis? Is this why you were asking me about him'

'Hear me out. They knew that I was booked to officiate at Dennis's funeral service and that I would be visiting you at some point to discuss the funeral arrangements. They wanted me to find out anything I can about his dealings. It was them who made me call you yesterday to arrange this appointment. Apparently Dennis was part of or had something to do with whatever was about to go down and when he died it meant they didn't get the information they were banking on him giving them. They didn't say what it was, but it was obviously important to them. They gave me a list of questions which they wanted me to include with mine when asking you about Dennis's life. You know, I was told to dig a bit deeper than I normally would when speaking to a bereaved spouse. Now it's obvious they haven't got a clue that we are an item, otherwise I wouldn't be standing here now and that gives us the advantage.'

'How so, I knew nothing of his lifestyle. I've done nothing wrong you've done nothing wrong so why should we need an advantage?'

He thinks, because I have a plan to escape and I'm about to lie through my teeth to get you to come with me.

'You must understand Lisa we need to keep a step ahead of these people, people who would most definitely try to involve you in Dennis's dealings. They're not going to walk away from this empty handed, they'll be looking for someone to take down. I bet they already have you marked as an accomplice or even worse. They're' bastards who I guarantee will stop at nothing. ' 'Oh my God, you really think so; I must not find myself in that situation. Why did you agree, I mean agree to help them, why?'

'They said that if I didn't co-operate they would arrest me on some trumped-up charges. That's what I mean, that's the sort of scum they are.'

'I guess that had it not been you Peter it would have been a different celebrant, who would have tried to trick me and all the time I would have been none the wiser, the fuckers, the irony of it all. Did they say which part of the police force they were connected to?'

'Human trafficking SCD9 Unit, whatever the fuck that means. Fuck Lisa what has Dennis been up to?'

'I don't know, how am I supposed to know? Are you sure they meant my Dennis because he wouldn't know anything about human trafficking?'

'Yes, they meant your Dennis alright. Look as I said we hold all the cards. We have the advantage and I promise I'll have them running round in circles in no time. So, this is what we will do.'

Back in their office, Grant and Guilford wait to hear from the surveillance team who are tracking North's comings and goings at Mortimer House.

'Christ Fay! He's been in there a long time, how long could it possibly take.'

'It's a good sign, if she had suspected something he would have been out on his ear by now. Relax, let him work his magic.'

'Surveillance reported that he wasn't searched at the gate. We should have wired him up just as we had originally planned to.'

'We discussed that as only being an option Paul and it was deemed to be too risky for him. We need North to be himself, natural like, not worried about carrying a wire. The success of 'Operation Lost Souls' rests solely with him now.'

Guilford gets a update from surveillance

'Paul, North has just left and is heading back to his apartment.'

'And about bloody time too!'

Chapter 32

Lisa Forrester makes a long distance phone call on a burner cell phone that she keeps taped to the back of a handmade wardrobe. It takes two connecting rings for it to be answered.

'Polanski.'

'Polanski, I now know who's been leaking information.'

'Who boss?

'My fucking late rat of a husband, that's who, he's been making deals with the fucking authorities, can you believe it? It sounds like he was about to pass them info which would have took us all down? What the fuck could he have been thinking? Some good news though, they have no idea it's me who's running the play. Tell me Polanski, those men who we suspected of being leaks, what's their status.'

'Dead'

'Fuck….Polanski, everything that I've just told you, you never heard, you understand?'

'Sure Boss.'

'Keep it to yourself. It's bad for business and morale.'

'You got it. Boss, can I ask a question?'

'Go ahead.'

'How did you find out, I mean about your husband?'

'Another time, let's just say a little fucking bird told me. Now that the leak has been fixed, permanently fixed, I've got plans I need to put into motion. I'll be in contact, and Polanski.'

'Yes boss.'

'The dead men, make sure their families don't go hungry.'

'You got it Boss.'

*

Guilford receives another update from surveillance. She puts the call on loud speaker.

'North has just arrived back at the apartment block. Hold for update.... an unknown male is approaching North's vehicle, he's getting into the passenger side, over.'

'Did you manage to get a description of the unknown, over?'

'Negative.'

Mayfair opens the passenger door of North's Jag and gets in.'

'Hey! What the fuck Mayfair! Haven't you heard of knocking first?'

'Stop fucking with me North, drive on and be quick about it.''

'Drive! Drive where for fuck sake?'

'The crematorium of course, where it's quiet now get going.'

'Who the hell can that be Fay? Surely it's not one of Forrester's goons.'

'Could be Paul, if that's the case and he's been rumbled, he could be in some sort of danger. Try his mobile.'

Grant makes the call. It goes to answer he tries again, same response.

'Right, Paul, I want to know who the fuck that person is and where they're going.'

Another update is patched through from surveillance.

'Vehicle entering the grounds of Portsmouth Crematorium, over.'

'Surveillance this is DI Guilford, our man might have been compromised and may need your assist but only on my say so. Keep me up-dated.

North parks in the almost empty carpark.

'I take it you've got the money?'

'It's in the glovebox.'

'All of it?'

'All of it.'

Mayfair turns the release catch on the glovebox, it drops open. He takes out a large white envelope, opens it and looks inside, he inhales deeply.

'The smell of money, man it's better than any woman, well any of the women I've ever known! I take it my bonus is in here too?'

'Your share has an elastic band around it.'

'Excellent, Mrs Maxwell will be pleased. Tell me man, how do you do it? You know, get her to hand that amount of cash over to you, I bet it's not just because you're a sweet talker, good-looking and you just happen to be there in her hour of need. My guess is you were fucking her getting the most out of her before moving on to the next widow or should I say victim,' Mayfair laughs. 'Peter, Peter, Peter, haven't you ever heard the saying about a woman scorned! Well then, Mr Peter North, it's been a pleasure doing business with you man, goodbye, I think I'll walk it from here.'

North places his hand on Mayfair's arm, stopping him from leaving.

'Mayfair, I'm going to put a proposition your way. There's money in it.'

'Ok spit it out, speak to me man. Look I'm cool, you're cool right.'

The surveillance team slowly drive past North's car. Cameras, which are hidden from view by tinted windows, click rapidly, capturing images of both North and his passenger.

'Patching through images now, all's quiet, continuing our surveillance.'

Grant and Guilford study the images.

'Paul I've seen this black guy before.'

Guilford reaches a folder containing the images that were taken outside J.C. Funeral Services. She spreads them out on the desk and points to one.

'There he is! It's John Mayfair the private eye who was caught on camera going into J.C. Funeral Services. I knew I'd seen him before.'

'Mayfair must be connected to the Forrester clan Fay, otherwise what's he doing at J.C. Funeral Services? If North does know him and he in turn knew Forrester then North is playing us like a fiddle.'

'If that's the case Paul, then we're well and truly fucked.'

Update from surveillance 'Unknown is out of vehicle and leaving by foot. North's driving off. Will continue surveillance, do you still want us to bring North in?'

'Damn sure we fucking well do, if he deviates from the route back to his apartment stop and apprehend him, otherwise wait till he gets there. Do we have surveillance on the unknown?'

'Negative.'

'Fuck, put a description of Mayfair out to the other units.'

'Fay, what is that fucker North up to?'

'Don't know but we'll soon find out.'

Surveillance calls in that North has now arrived at his apartment. Guilford eventually gets through to North's mobile telling him that a car will be there to pick him up ASAP.

Chapter 33

A SCD9 officer takes North to the same interview room as before. He sits tapping rhythms out on the table as he waits for Guilford and Grant to arrive. It doesn't take them long.

'Fuck North, you were in that house a long, long time.'

'These things take time, it's delicate, it can be a highly emotionally charged situation and not to be rushed. Not your forte I imagine, DS Grant.'

'So! Speak to us. What was said, how did it go?'

'Fay, it's going to take time for her to digest, mull over the questions I put to her. It's not uncommon for someone in a state of bereavement. She said that her husband kept a diary which he would look at occasionally for names, places and dates.' He thinks, that's got your interest hasn't it you assholes. 'So really, at this moment in time, all I have got is just the bog standard info that most families give me, that's if I'm lucky to get any at all! Families usually have little or nothing to say, leaving it up to me and other celebrants to produce a eulogy out of scraps of information.'

'We'll read through your notes anyway and we'll need to get our hands on that diary.' I thought you would assholes.

'Regarding the diary, she didn't give any indication as to its whereabouts. So I'm hoping all will be revealed during my next visit.'

'Peter you did well but is there something you're not telling us, like are you holding out on us?'

'Holding out on you? Not sure I know what you mean there.'

'What if I told you that we know you've not been straight with us?'

North feels agitated. He thinks, do these fuckers know about me and Lisa. No, not possible, they would have jumped on me the minute they walked through that door closely followed by a call to Fraud to take me away.

'Not being straight with you, Fay, I don't understand.'

'Well Peter, we know for sure you didn't go straight home after leaving the Forrester's residence. That was the plan, wasn't it, to go straight back to your apartment?'

Realising he hasn't been rumbled, that this has nothing to do with his relationship with Lisa Forrester he relaxes.

'I did drive back to my apartment block, didn't go in though, had a change of mind, I drove to the crematorium.'

'Why?'

'It's personal'

Guilford lays a photo of him and Mayfair in his Jag on the table.

'So, tell us, who is he.'

'Really you two, is this important?'

'Well we think so. We have him going in and out of J.C. Funeral Services, you see we think he could be part of the Forrester set-up and yet he seems to know you pretty well. So, just as one and one is two, you and this guy add up to you are fucking us over.'

'You've got it so wrong, both of you. He doesn't fucking know them from shit. He went in there looking for me.'

'And why would he be looking for you?'

'Like I said it's personal. His name's John Mayfair and he's a private detective. Look him up you'll find I'm telling the truth.'

'Well shit Peter, it would seem that you've got all the men and their dogs looking for you. By the way, we knew about Mayfair, just seeing if you are prepared to be up front with us. So come on tell, what did you two talk about, surly not the fucking fucking weather?'

'Look Grant, you stupid fuck, I handed him over some money that I owed a client of his. It was no big deal. It's all over and done with, no connection whatsoever to your case.'

'Me the stupid fuck, that's a joke North, aren't your clients supposed to pay you instead you pay them?'

'You wouldn't understand, shit for brains. I wouldn't double-cross you guys, we've got a deal going remember, I'm upholding my part and I expect you to do the same.'

'Come on you two will you just drop it? Peter, before your next visit to Mrs Forrester you will be brought back here so we can brief you on what we expect of you. In the meantime, if I dare say it, carry on as usual, and Peter, you will remain under tight surveillance. That's it. A car will take you back to your apartment.'

Chapter 34

Back in his apartment North calls Lisa Forrester. He puts it on loud speaker.

'Hi Lisa its Peter I said that you wouldn't recognise the number, it's a throw-away, a burner. Those bastards had my mobile in their possession for some time, before giving it back to me. I imagine they have fucked with it with some sort of device. Are you ok?'

'Yes I guess so. It's hard you know. Anyway did you have any luck with Mayfair?'

'I got to see him sooner than I thought I would! But yes, He's a bad boy and a risk taker, especially if it involves money. I kept a lot of info back from him though, just ran it through sketchy like.'

'And how did it go with, did you call them the SCD9 Unit? Something like that, anyway how did it go?'

'Right first time, they were totally sucked in by the whole story I spun them and they want to see me before I visit you again. Lisa love I know you're going through it big time at the moment and my heartfelt thoughts are with you.'

'Thank you Peter for being here I don't know what I would do without you, you know, for loving me and warning me of those bastards intentions.'

'So, we will finalise our plan over the next few days. Keep this number on redial.'

'I will and I will work on what we discussed. Must go now, I've got family around, be in touch with you, love you bye.'

'Love you too babe, bye.'

After hanging up, Lisa Forrester looks down at her phone and starts to laugh.

'Peter, you really are a fucking moron, do you really think I'm some sort of dumb loved-up idiot.'

On the day of his second visit North is driven from his apartment and taken to SCD9 headquarters and is met at reception by Grant and Guilford. Once more he is taken to the same interview room.

'Hope you've managed to keep a low profile since we last met Peter?'

'Well Fay you two should know! By the way, hope my tail enjoyed the funeral service I gave at the crematorium yesterday, must have been really exciting for whoever had that job. As for bugs and cameras in my apartment I wouldn't put that past you lot.'

Guilford blushes, 'I can assure you Peter that no surveillance of any description has been placed in your apartment.'

'That's good to know. My love life is X-rated stuff, the thought of you guys having front row tickets, well, that can affect a man's performance you know.'

Grant is pissed off at even the suggestion.

'Believe me North we aren't interested in that kind of shit so shut your mouth.'

'For fuck sake can't you two just stop it and focus on what we are here for. Peter, it's imperative that you begin to get answers especially about the whereabouts of the diary.'

'I'll try my best Fay but in the end it's down to whatever info she's prepared to give me, and not any reflection on me.'

'Here take this.'

Guilford hands him a folded piece of paper which he opens and reads.

'We want you to drop these names into your conversation, make a mental note to what her reaction is to each of names.'

'Ok that's easily done.'

'Getting hold of that diary is a priority though.'

'Consider it done, by the way Fay, when do you intend to hand me over to Fraud?'

'When the funeral service is over and done with and don't worry, you will have time to put your house in order and I will negotiate good terms for you.'

'Thanks Fay, depending on you. But you do realise that my job as a celebrant isn't over until I've attended the wake, it's where I'm expected to share a few words that are on a more personal level with the deceased's family.

'I didn't realise but if that's the case then so be it, if you're not out soon after everyone has left we will withdraw our deal.'

'Understood, I just want to do what's best for the family you know.'

*

Cold Case Fraud Officer Detective Inspector Smyth meets with her team, Officers Devon, Baines and Khair.

'As you can appreciate it's been a major blow and bloody frustrating to say the least, having to be kept away from North. Still I'd like to know how SCD9 managed to get to him before we did.'

'You know what I reckon?'

'What's that Devon?'

'Well SCD9 may have planned this all along you know, play him off us to gain North's trust, get some kind of deal going, so he could help them in one way or another.'

'Exactly my thoughts too Devon.'

Baines interjects, 'If that's the case then the DCI hasn't been up front with us.'

'Look you lot I know the boss and he wouldn't...'

'I'm not so sure.'

'Why so Baines?'

'Didn't you say that the DCI was hot on building close relationships between departments, sharing intelligence, cooperating across the board etc.'

'Look you three, drop it. As far as I'm concerned we can link North to a possible dozen cases of fraudulent activities and he's going down big time. We need this bust, this unit needs it to prove its worth, or we are going to be closed down,' Guilford

158

points across to the main building. 'I can assure you that there are those across there who think we are a waste of Division's money and time and would like nothing better than to see this unit shut down and I have my suspicions to how SCD9 got to North before us.'

Chapter 35

The heavens open as Peter North drives up to the main gates of the Forrester's property, He partly lowers his window. The same security guard as before walks over to him, this time wearing a hooded raincoat. He scrolls through his mobile phone, which is covered in a transparent watertight membrane, before taking another hard look at North. The electronic gate opens. He waves him through.

'Drive on sir.'

North parks in the same parking area as on his previous visit. In an attempt not to get too wet he makes a dash to the entrance of the house. After being let in by one of the housemaids he is shown to the same room as before. He finds Lisa pacing up and down. She hurries over to him, they hold each other closely.

'Oh Peter! We are doing the right thing aren't we?'

'Hey love it's the best we can do, our options are limited.'

They sit down on one of the settees.

'Lisa, it's all arranged at my end, have you managed to finalise yours?'

'Yes but it took some doing.'

'Then all we have to do now is wait it out and for everyone to do their part when the time comes.'

'What about Mayfair, are you sure he will do his?'

'Believe me Lisa, when a guy like Mayfair gets the smell of money they kind of stick to it like shit to a shovel. You know what! Why don't we let the housekeeper know that her services are no longer required for the rest of the afternoon? I need you real bad babe!'

*

The office of SCD9 Special Unit

'I guess it's going to be ages again before we hear from North, he's been in there, what, two hours already? We should

160

have wired him this time Fay. He didn't get the shakedown on his first visit and he didn't this time, I ...'

'Paul as I said Peter's doing okay, he's obviously busy.'

'Peter's doing okay! I hope I'm not sensing a bit of something going on here between you two?'

'No way Paul, you should know better than to say that. And anyway, if that were the case, I wouldn't be throwing him out just because he got some crumbs in the bed.'

'And what if told you I eat toast in bed, do you think...'

'Hell no, don't you even go there. I bet your wife would moan like fuck if you left crumbs in the bed and that's way after kicking you out!'

'Ok, ok I get it, just joking, I'm no Peter North.' He looks at his watch. 'How long is he fucking going to be?'

Chapter 36

North gets ready to leave Mortimer House.

'So Lisa, this is it, next time we meet will be on the day of the Service.' North holds her in his arms.

'Look at me Lisa, look me in the eyes, are you sure you're up for this?

'Yes I'm sure.' She thinks of course I am you dumb fuck I need a way out of here, you're offering me a more exciting way out, so why not, it'll be fun. I can always cut and run, and do it my way.'

'Lisa as long as we all do and say the right things we'll be fine.'

'Peter, as far as I'm concerned the sooner this business is all over and done with the better. In fact I'm looking forward to it just being us, you and me, away from here.'

'Lisa you know they're going to be questioning me about this visit but don't worry, I've got it covered.'

'Promise me you won't overplay your hand, I don't want either of us to end up in prison.' He thinks, she's really has fallen for this. The stupid bitch but I love her.'

'It won't come to that, I promise.'

As North arrives at the main gate the security man acknowledges him and waves him through.

Guilford receives notification from surveillance that North has now left the premises.

Grant calls North's mobile phone.

'North, maintain a steady speed, one of our unmarked cars will be with you soon so keep close and follow.'

It's not long before an unmarked car pulls alongside North's. Its driver signals the thumbs up sign, then points forward indicating that he, North, is to follow. The unmarked car accelerates and takes its position in front. North follows as they turn off the main road onto a country lane. Reaching an area of farmland they park next to a derelict farmhouse and walk across its yard to a large black van. The side door is opened from inside, North steps in.

Guilford and Grant are there to welcome him. He sees that the van is decked out with Hi-Tec equipment: close-circuit TVs, computers, radio-phones and aerial images of what he assumes is Forrester's estate.

'Welcome to our Bat Mobile Peter! Take a seat.'

'Very impressive set-up you have here Fay. Somewhat similar to what we used in the Special Forces.'

'Technologies moved on a bit since then North.'

North thinks, you really are an ass-hole Grant.

'Is that right Grant, I wouldn't have guessed,' he thinks, you shit-head.

'So, looks like you have all the angles covered Fay.'

'You could say that, the only exception would be internal surveillance and the rear of the property can be a bit patchy at times.' He thinks, interesting.

'Well then, nothing's changed that much, has it Grant! You know, you've got all this Hi-Tec and you've still got to rely on the likes of me. Fay, I suppose you've tried bugging the place and failed.'

'Dennis Forrester was too astute to let that happen, believe me we tried. All his staff was handpicked and vetted by him personally. He made a point of letting them know he knew the names of their husbands, their wives, children, and if they fucked up, well you get the message.'

'Nice guy our Mr Forrester! Ok, so, I take it you want to know how I got on during my visit?'

'I've been meaning to ask North, purely out of curiosity you understand, do you like toast!'

DI Guilford looks at DS Grant, she rolls her eyes up.

'Do I what!'

'Take no notice of him Peter. Anyway, moving on, the diary, have you been able to confirm that there is an actual diary and if so its location in the house?'

'She's got one alright, a black leather-bound one, pages filled with dates, addresses, names and some loose receipts.'

'Did you see where she kept it?'

'Not at first Fay, it was already open on a table amongst some other paperwork when I arrived but I did however manage to see where she put it and that was in a wall safe. I made a mental note of the combination number when she opened it to put the diary and papers back in. As the safe door was opened I noticed there were a few bundles of banknotes, a set of keys and a number of passports.'

'And can you remember the number sequence?'

'That's what I said.'

Grant pushes a note pad and pen across the table.

'Here, write it down.'

'That's not going to happen. Look, it's in my head and that's where it's going to stay. It's my insurance, don't worry I'll make sure I get the diary alright.'

'Have some fucking faith in us North. Bloody ironic don't you think Fay?'

'What's that?'

'North, making out to be a celebrant and being told to get some faith. What a joke.'

'You're right you ass-hole, I have no faith. Only a belief in myself and the ability to...'

Grant cuts in. 'What to defraud defenceless grieving women.'

'Fuck you. I tell you what, you're lucky you've got me. I'm the golden ticket! I'm the one who can get you out of the shit you're in, so watch your mouth you fuck or I'll fill it in with my fist.'

Grant takes a boxer's stance. 'Come on then tough guy let me see what they taught you in the Forces.'

'What, with all this expensive equipment in here, you fucking moron. Let's take this outside and listen, you're going to regret ever saying what you did because I'm about to teach you to keep that fat big fucking mouth of yours shut. And when I've finished, you can all go fuck yourselves, I'll take my chances with Fraud. Now step outside and let's get this over and done with.'

North's physicality seemed to have doubled in size, exuding menace. Grant's heart starts to pound in his chest, his blood pressure thumps in his head, making him feel light-headed. He is more than relieved when an armed security officer positions himself in front of the vans door stopping them both from leaving.

Guilford pushes her way in between them 'What is it with you two? I'm sick and tired of you two locking horns. Just pack it in, for fuck sakes!'

'Well then Fay tell your fat headed pig here, your deluded colleague to keep the fuck off my back or I will crush him and your shit case will collapse around your ears.'

To help save face, Grant displays an act of false bravado by ordering the armed officer to step aside from the door, knowing, of course that the armed officer would not do so unless directed by Guilford and that wasn't likely to happen.

'Paul, let it go and do as North says, I believe he would seriously harm you and I bet he more than likely could. I mean it's a total mismatch.'

Grant feeling highly relieved at the prospect of not having to face North off, retreats to the back of the van and focusses on regulating his breathing and getting his heart rate down.

'OK, you two keep it together. Peter, I've written down a number for you to call if you need to get in touch with us urgently.'

She hands him a note.

'I was about to ask you about that just before that big fat fuck summoned up some courage to take me on. Thanks Fay.'

Grant looks away.

North folds the note and puts it in the inner pocket of his suit jacket.

Grant dares to catch North's attention.

'I want to say something North.'

'Fay tell this shit I'm not interested in what he's got to say will ya.'

'No wait, hear me out, apologies for my outburst, man. Look we're all under pressure here. You're about to conduct a funeral service, steal from a safe and infiltrate a criminal's house all on our behalf and here I'm giving you grief. Look I'm sorry man, I should have known better. I've got to hand it to you North, so thanks again. Keep that number Fay gave you close at all times, one of us will be on the other end.

Chapter 37

2.15pm Wednesday 15th November.

Mourners are waiting outside the chapel at Portsmouth Crematorium readying themselves for the imminent arrival of the Funeral cars. North is inside the chapel checking to make sure everything is in place and having a final scan through the service notes.

From out of one of the stained glass windows of the chapel, he sees the funeral procession approaching and makes his way outside and positions himself in front of the Chapel's doors, his hands down by his side and looking forward, as if he was at attention. As the hearse carrying Forrester's coffin slowly creeps past North and comes to a standstill, he bows in respect. Funeral director James Clifton and four of his assistants get out of the hearse and make their way to its rear. Lisa accompanied by three family members, gets out of the following limousine as some late arrivals make their way across from the car park.

James Clifton and North approach Lisa and share some quiet comforting words with her. Clifton returns to the hearse then, with a nod of his head, the poll bearers skilfully and smoothly slide the coffin from out of the rear of the hearse and on to their shoulders. Led by North, James Clifton and four bearers slowly make their way into the chapel. The music '*Nimrod*' by Edward Elgar fills the chapel. Lisa and the other mourners follow behind. All is being captured on cameras by the SCD9 surveillance team.

Funeral service ends: 3pm

Family and friends gather outside the chapel most remarking how lovely the service was and how much Dennis will be missed. North makes his way through the large crowd of mourners to Lisa. Before he reaches her Zara Maxwell steps out in front of him.

'Zara!'

167

'Peter. Well, this is awkward don't you know.' He thinks, you fucking bitch, pissed as usual I guess,'

'Zara I hope you can forget what happened and have managed to put it behind you.'

'Hell yes, it's all water under the bridge thanks to Mayfair. Just one thing though, if you mess with my dearest friend Lisa like you messed with me, well, your miserable life won't be worth living, hope you understand.'

'Look you don't have to worry about that.' He thinks, fuck you bitch.

'Just make sure you keep it that way.' He thinks, I should have made you suffer. I might still.

As North walks away Maxwell calls after him.

'Oh and Peter, just one more thing.'

North cringes at the thought of what might come out of her mouth. He walks back to her so she doesn't find the need to shout out whatever it is she's going to say.

'And what's that Zara?'

'A lovely service,' He stares at her thinking you fucking bitch, piss-head.

North catches up with Lisa. They quietly stroll for a while in the grounds of the crematorium.

'You ok Lisa?'

'Very sad but yes I am. Do you think they have been watching us, the police that is?'

He thinks that pisshead Maxwell certainly will be.

'They most probably are Lisa. I imagine they've recorded everyone who's turned up which they will try and match against their list of known criminals.'

'Won't they think it suspicious us talking to one another, out here on our own?

He thinks, no, but that bitch Maxwell will.

'I doubt it Lisa, to them it's me just doing my job, guessing I'm saying some words of comfort to the widow.'

'Heartless that's what they are Peter, bloody heartless. It's all back to my place for the wake I guess. I'm ready to get things going, all or nothing hey!'

3.45

Family and friends arrive back at Mortimer House. The security is tighter than normal making the process slow for getting into the grounds. Most vehicles park in the parking area whilst others pull up on the grass verge. Abandoning their cars they make their way to the main entrance of the house where they are greeted by two uniformed servants offering glasses of freshly poured Champagne served on silver trays. Once inside everyone is free to roam in and out of the rooms on the ground floor level, introducing themselves to one another and as they do so, admiring the furnishings and décor of this lavish house.

Chapter 38

Late Afternoon

DI Guilford gets an up-date from the surveillance team out.

'All persons parked up and accounted for and now in the main house, over.'

'Well Paul, that's that, now all we can do is wait it out. Have you been in contact with Fraud to let them know that they will be able to pick North up later this afternoon?'

'No, I left that with the DCI, it will be a chance for her to showcase better communication across the various forces. She wouldn't like us to steal the limelight.'

'That's so considerate of you, you creep!'

'I guess then we'll know when the handover is going to happen just as long as they know it's going to be later than they thought.'

'I'll put a good word in for him.'

'Fay, he's going to expect more than a good word, otherwise we are going to have one pissed off celebrant, and increase our chances of going to hell. Look, it's not as if he was even religious was it. He saw a niche in the funeral market and exploited it, end of.'

'But he has, and is still trying doing his best to help us out.'

'Oh come on Fay, he's only doing this to save his own skin, to lessen any charges Fraud might throw at him.'

'Face it Paul, without him we'd be no further forward than we were before he came on to the scene and all those innocent people in the grips of that gang waiting to be trafficked, well, you could have kissed them goodbye. No, he deserves a medal if you ask me, not to be sold down the river. He needs better representation before being handed over to fraud.'

'For fuck sake Fay, listen to yourself.'

'No Paul, fuck you, I'm going to call it in to the DCI. It wasn't that long ago you were praising him for his help now you want to throw him to the dogs, face it you've disliked him from the get go.'

'Ok I admit it the arrogant bastard, but you, you've been infatuated by him from the beginning. I'm good at reading people Fay and boy you're an easy read, he has sucked you in good and proper.'

'Well if that's what you think…'

'It's not what I think it's what I know. I happened to be driving through the area where he lives and who was it I saw drive around to the rear of the property, it was you. Curiosity got the better of me so I U-turned and followed. I kept on following you on foot when you went into the building. I stopped stood there in the shadows by the rear of the elevator and watched you go up to his apartment and don't deny it. Now some time back I questioned you about your involvement with him and you said there was nothing in it, just some guy you met at the gym. I gave you the benefit of the doubt and left it at that. So, tell me straight Fay, what the fucks going on?'

'OK, ok you're right it was more than that, but not at the beginning not when you first asked. I liked him at first, of course I did. Since we brought him in I've got to know him better. There was chemistry there and yes you are right I was infatuated by him. Going to his apartment had nothing to do whatsoever with the case. I needed to get him out of my system and that's all it was.'

'So you screwed him.'

'Well…yes.'

'For fuck sake Fay you've just about broke every rule in the book.'

'Look because of the way I felt for him he didn't benefit from it, I mean in terms of the case.'

'No, you just fucked him instead.'

'The once, no more, he has his woman, Mia from the Swan, he doesn't want anything to do with the likes of me.'

'What do you mean?'

'Oh, come on, think about it, me working for the police, much too complicated for him. To him I was just a fuck to me he was just a fuck, end of story'

'Ok I get it but I feel fucking let down Fay, fucking let down I tell you. You're better than this.'

'Paul, I know it's a lot to ask but can we please draw a line under this and move on.'

'I don't know, fuck I don't know....Can you give me some assurance that this sort of shit won't happen again because if it wasn't me and it was someone else you'd have been reported by now and bang, end of your career. But you know what, we need people like you who are dedicated to the cause so yeah forget it but if I get any hint of anything going on between you two again or with any future suspect, I will have no option but to report you.'

'It will never happen again Paul, I can assure you.'

Chapter 39

Across one of the lavishly decorated rooms of Mortimer House, North catches Lisa's eye, he nods suggesting she follows him out. Lisa ends her conversation with a group of family members, excuses herself and makes her way to the large conservatory where North is waiting.

'It will soon be time to leave Lisa, are you all set?'

'I've packed the essentials and sorted all my financial transactions.'

'And your ESTA?'

'Yes all taken care of.'

'Great, I need to make that call to Mayfair, Ok for me to pop upstairs where it's more private?'

'Sure, I'll get back to family and friends, strange though and upsetting that I won't be able to say goodbye to them properly but all for the best hey.'

*

5pm

North makes his way upstairs and enters a bedroom. He walks over to one of the big bay windows where he stands, staring out at the low November sun, collecting his thoughts. A shiver runs through him bringing him back to the job in hand. He calls Mayfair who is waiting in the indoor swimming pool.

*

Earlier that day: 2pm leading up to the funeral service.

Peter North parks in the busy grounds of Portsmouth Crematorium. With his black leather zip-up folder containing the service notes to Dennis Forrester's funeral service, he leaves his car unlocked and walks towards the chapel. Mayfair, who's been waiting in the carpark, makes his way to North's Jag, keeping low so as not to be seen by surveillance. He opens the rear nearside door and lies across the black leather back seat and remains there hidden out of sight.

*

After the funeral service as finished North makes his way back inside the chapel to collect his briefcase then returns to his car. The smell of stale aftershave and cigarette smoke confirmed that Mayfair as planed is inside.

Mayfair starts yawning. 'Hey man! That's the best sleep I've had in ages.'

'Just keep your head down Mayfair, we're about to leave and join the procession of vehicles going back for the wake.'

'I'm keeping down man don't you worry. Don't suppose there's any coffee back here? Just kidding!'

'OK, here we go, we're off. Regarding the rest of your money, you'll be contacted by a third party to let you know when and where to collect it, which of course, depends on me giving the third party the go ahead and that will only happen when your part in this is over.'

'That's fine by me man. I trust you and I'm sure you wouldn't want to cross me.'

'Just try and get comfortable and make sure you cover yourself as best as you can with that blanket back there, I'll let you know when we are getting close. Security is tight and surveillance will be watching. Look, I'm going to run the plan through with you once more just to finalise things so we both know the score.'

'I'm all ears.'

North thinks you fucking better be.

'So, when we arrive and parked up, I'll be leaving my mobile, there's a tracking device in it but it's nothing for you to worry about and I'll leave the keys in the ignition then I'll make my way to the house. You give it a minute or two before getting out, making sure you keep a low profile by using the guests as cover. When nearing the house breakaway and make your way

174

to the building which is an indoor swimming pool, it's the building I pointed out to you on the map to the right of the main house. When you get there you will find the door unlocked. Make yourself at home and I will call you nearer the time. Is that clear?'

'Yeah I'm cool man.'

'Now for the rest, your turn, run it by me.'

'Shit man, it's hard enough to breathe back here never mind talk. He pulls the blanket away from his face. Okay, one of Forrester's maids, Jenny, who has already been briefed and paid up front, will at some point join me in the indoor pool. You will call on your burner to make sure all is okay then call again when the show's about to go on the road. We get into the Jag and drive away, along any road as long as it's heading north bound.'

'And don't forget Mayfair, you will be under surveillance. The moment you leave the premises you will be followed, hence the mobile phone with its tracker, and eventually stopped but hopefully that won't be until at least an hour or so has passed. So, having been stopped, how are you going to cover your ass?'

'That we've been hired to drive your car to, well, nowhere special, just out for a drive, now where's the crime in that Officer! Look, I'm good, you can rely on me. Man, have you got this sussed or what, I always knew there was more to you than meets the eye. You have the smell of military about you.'

'I've fought in every shit-hole imaginable and survived. This is just a walk in the park. Most of the time you're only as good as your back-up and Mayfair you're my back-up, so make it good.'

'Yes Sir!'

*

Present time.

From one of the lavish bedrooms of Mortimer House, North calls Mayfair.

'Mayfair, just checking everything is ok.'

'Smooth, it's a big pool should have brought me budgie smugglers! But yes everything's in place. I'm on stand-by for your next call.'

North makes his way back downstairs and mingles with family and friends of the late Dennis Forrester. North catches Lisa's attention by nodding and mouthing words, indicating that all is well, She acknowledges with a knowing look, one he knows so well.

*

There is a gentle tapping on the door to the swimming pool, it begins to slowly open. Mayfair stands back into the shadows and the flickering shapes of light and shade given off by the underwater lighting of the swimming pool. The visitor peers in.

'Hello, anyone in there?'

Mayfair steps out of the shadows.

'Oh Jesus, you made me jump!'

'Quick, come in and close the door. I take it you're Jenny,'

'Yes.'

'Well then Jenny, make yourself at home. There's some food and drink if you're interested.'

'No thanks I don't think I could manage anything right now.'

'It shouldn't be too long now. Don't suppose you know what all this is about, I doubt they would have told you.'

'Look as far as I'm concerned I'm just along for the ride and that's all I want to know.'

'Let me guess why you were chosen.' Mayfair looks her up and down. 'It wouldn't be because you look like Mrs Forrester would it!' he laughs.

'Well I guess there are similarities in the way we look yes but she's much more attractive than I am but that's what having money can do for you.'

'Why you do yourself a disservice.' Remembering back to when he first met Joan Maxwell, Mayfair laughs. recalling that's not the first time he's heard those words.

Mayfair's attention is quickly drawn to the far end of the swimming pool as beams of torchlight dance around as a door is being opened, He pulls Jenny into the shadows then into a small cubicle and puts his hand over her mouth.

'Sssh,' he whispers. 'keep quiet and keep still.' He slowly removes his hand from her mouth and places his index finger to his lips. 'Sssh.'

The sound of the two approaching voices and footsteps bounce around the building.

'See they didn't put the cover over it then Jed.'

'Think they had some sort of pool party here yesterday Mike, in fact I'm pretty sure they did, I saw it on yesterday's security rota when I signed in this evening.'

'That'll explain it then Jed,'

Mike shines the beam of his torch on the tray of food that had been left for Mayfair. 'Don't know why those sandwiches have been left there Jed, they still look fresh to me, might even help myself to one of those later, you know, to satisfy those early hour hunger pains.'

'I wouldn't Mike, you don't know who's been at them. Anyway, come on we've got the perimeter to check out yet.'

Both men leave the building.

'Man that was a close call.'

'Do you think they have gone?'

'Wait here, I'll check it out.'

Mayfair stealthily makes his way along the pool's edge, ducking low under each of the five windows. The door the men came through and left by was shut. He peered through one of the windows and could see the beam from one of the men's torches disappear as they turn the corner of another building. He makes his way back to the cubicle where Jenny is waiting.

'It's ok, they've gone you can come out now.'

'God I was so scared I thought that...'

'Jenny, relax, it sounds like they won't be back for some time, the early hours by the way they spoke.'

'If you say so.'

'Yep I do and before we leave here I'm going to mess with their heads by hiding this food in the cubicle thus leaving Mike and Jed pondering over some empty trays!'

Chapter 40

As the guests leave Mortimer House, Lisa stands at the main door thanking everyone for their support and for attending the funeral service. Meanwhile North calls Mayfair to let him know it's on.

'Mayfair they're leaving, good luck.'

'It's been good knowing you man, maybe bump into each other some other time, some other place and hey, Peter, take care of yourself.'

North reaches into his inside pocket for the folded piece of paper that Guilford gave him. He dials. Guilford answers, Grant listens in.

'Peter.'

'Fay, I've just learnt that all the contents of the house safe have been moved to a warehouse. Where exactly, I don't know, but the good news is she's asked me to drive her there. So, I still have a good chance of getting hold of the diary, we're leaving now.'

'Shit, shit!.... Ok Peter you've done good. We've got no choice but to roll with it.'

'Grant here North, we'll be keeping close, you can rely on that.'

North thinks, that's exactly what I planned for you, you fucking jerk.

'Well that's comforting to know, you ass-hole. I wouldn't want it any other way!' North disconnects.

'Fay, how many warehouses do we know of that belonged to Forrester?'

'Three.'

'We should get some of our people to cover those ASAP.'

Having seen the last visitor out, Lisa closes the front door turns, and sees North coming down the stairs. 'All clear Lisa?'

'Yes everyone's gone.'

'Then let's do it.'

Mayfair and Jenny, make their way from the swimming pool to North's car. As planned the keys are waiting in the ignition. He places the mobile phone in an inside pocket of the door and begins driving out of Mortimer House. Mayfair positions the car in between two visitors' SUV's to cut down the chance of being identified.

An up-date is patched through to Guilford and Grant who are waiting inside the surveillance van.

'North and Forrester have just left the premises and they're heading north. The helicopter will relay North's' position to you, over.'

'Ok Paul, we're on!'

'Fay, we don't know of any warehouses that Forrester has in the north, so don't you think it's a bit strange that...'

'What?'

'Nothing Fay, let's go'.

*

North and Forrester make their way out of the rear of the Mortimer House. The sound of a helicopter disappearing in the distance confirms to North that Mayfair is being followed. They continue along the sloping garden path that leads down to a jetty where they board a waiting boat and are welcomed aboard by the Captain. North and Forrester make their way inside the cabin and in no time at all they are speeding towards the open sea and Europe.

'That's it Lisa, we've done it!'

'Yes Peter, we've done it, well, so far at least, but it's not over, we both have very long roads to travel.'

'That sounds ominous, like we're parting company or something.'

'We are. Listen to me, I made it my business to know all about you from the first day we met, the womanising, the defrauding, I know it all. And that shit you fed me about me being nabbed by the Human Exploitation team was all bull shit!'

'And yet you went along with it, why? Was it just for me?'

'No not just for you, wake up and smell the roses, it was for me. After what you told me I needed to get away, you had a good plan so I went along with it.'

'Hold on, you needed to get away after hearing what I had to say, why? Away from what for fuck sake.'

'The SCD9, The Human Exploitation team of course, that's who. Anything that you had found out about Dennis and his associates would have ruined me. I would have been locked up and they would have thrown away the key.'

'Ruined you? Locked up? How, why? '

'Unknown to them and to you my dear Peter, is that's it's me who organises and runs the human trafficking racket between Europe and England. Dennis played a big part in it, of course he did, but he did what he was told. Don't you see, for fuck sake Peter, it was me, I was the missing part. I was the information that Dennis was about to hand over to those bastards. I never suspected but they must have had him in their clutches for some time, there had been too many leaks in the organisation. He obviously made a deal where if he gave them the name of who was running the trafficking organisation along with contacts in Europe they would forget all about him. So no! I couldn't stay behind it was too fucking dangerous. It wouldn't have took them long to put two and two together. They never give up you see.'

'Fuck no! This is crazy! You involved in human trafficking, no fucking way!'

'In Europe I can continue with my work. I have money, lots of it and connections. My people are waiting for me to arrive, you can be a part of it too we could do with a man with your military skills.'

'Lisa I take my hat off to you, fuck! You're one hell of a woman! But trafficking human beings into God knows what kind of life! No, I couldn't, I couldn't be a part of that, so just as well we will be going our separate ways. Never to be mentioned by me again, ever.'

'Can I have your word on that Peter?'

North knows his life hangs in the balance and that her men, some armed, could easily kill him and dispose of his body overboard. Who would know who would even care?

Chapter 41

Mayfair glances into his rear-view mirror and experience tells him that he is being followed.

'Come on you bastards make your move we don't want to be driving all night, Mr Holmes will need feeding.'

'You sure we're not going to get into any trouble doing this?'

'Relax Jenny, we're just out for a drive, where's the problem in that. Like I said, let me do all the talking. Meanwhile enjoy the journey,'

'Who is this Mr Holmes, a sick relative or something?'

Mayfair laughs. 'Mr Sherlock Holmes is my partner in battling crime! Jenny, Mr Holmes is the purrrrfect feline!'

'So, Mr Holmes is just a cat.'

'Yep, he's but a cat.'

The SCD9 surveillance team following North's car are overtaken by a black Range Rover. VRN identifies the vehicle as being registered to Fraud Squad. Surveillance patches the information through to Guilford and Grant, who are speeding with blue light and are not far behind.

'What the fuck is Fraud playing at Paul? They were told to wait and we would deliver North to them.'

'They're making sure they get their man. My guess is they must have been keeping tags on North since day one, we just didn't see it, fuck!'

'Paul, put your foot down, hard!'

Grant and Guilford soon have the SCD9 surveillance vehicle in their sights. Fraud's Range Rover makes its move drawing alongside North's Jag and DS Smyth indicates to the driver to pull over. Then, by powering on, they manoeuver themselves in front by intermittently braking hard they bring the Jag to a halt.

Above, the police helicopter's searchlight is focused on events that are happening on the ground. All four vehicles come to a halt. Those in pursuit leave their vehicles and run to North's Jag. Smyth gets there seconds before Grant and Guilford. Smyth goes to open the driver's door as Grant puts his hand on one of her shoulders and spins her around to face him. Her hair blowing wildly as it is caught in the downdraft caused by the rotor blades of the helicopter. They have to shout to be heard.

'You're Smyth from Fraud, what the fuck are you doing stopping this vehicle and what right do you have to be here anyway? This is an SCD9 operation.'

'No! The driver of this vehicle is Peter North and he is wanted for fraud, he's ours now so back off!'

'The fuck I will, Smyth you've overstepped your mark here, now fuck off!'

Guilford forces her way between them and the vehicle. She opens the driver's door.

'Stop, Just stop it both of you, it's not him, it's not North!'

Smyth and Grant are both taken aback. They say in unison 'What the fuck do you mean, it's not him.'

'I couldn't be any plainer, this is NOT! Peter North and she is NOT! Lisa Forrester, we've been fucking had, all of us.'

Smyth pushes Guilford to one side and looks into the car.

'Then who the fuck is this? And where the fuck is North?'

Grant bangs the roof of the vehicle with both hands. 'I'll tell you who the fuck this is Smyth,…John fucking Mayfair.'

'And who the fuck is John Mayfair!'

'Someone who's just made us look like bloody idiots!'

Mayfair shouts, 'Good evening Officers, a lovely evening for a drive don't you think! Although, these country roads do seem extremely busy for this time of the day, strangely enough, so do the skies!

'Paul, yes boss, for fucks sake radio through to that fucking chopper and tell it to get the fuck out of here now! I can hardly hear myself talk never mind think.'

Grant makes his way back to their vehicle and radios through the command.

Mayfair leans back into his seat and points across to his passenger.

'May I introduce my driving companion Jenny.'

'Say hello to these nice police folk Jenny.'

Jenny leans forward and looks across Mayfair towards Guilford and Smyth who are looking at her dumbfounded.

'Hello, nice to meet you.'

As the Police helicopter leaves the area all is quiet, all is still and apart from the interior light from North's car, the headlights and flashing blue lights from the other vehicles, all is dark.

Conclusion

9 Months later
    In a chapel: State of Wichita, Kansas, USA
    27th August 2020
    Captain O'Neil stands astride one of the fallen men and barks an order 'Now roll over face down and place both hands behind your back.' Under the cover of armed police officers and the police sniper, Captain O'Neil holsters his weapon, bends down on one knee and handcuffs him. Then, by grabbing him under both arms, pulls the man up to the kneeling position, his head is drooping forward and facing down. Meanwhile, the other man lies motionless, an officer checks for signs of life.....
    'Captain O'Neil, this one's dead.'
    'Ok mister, now listen to me, I want you to stand up. Do you understand?' 'Yes but I'm going to need your help, I'm hurting.'
    Handcuffed from behind, the fallen man struggles to stand. Captain O'Neil helps pull him up and steadies him when he is completely upright. He turns his blooded captive around to face him.

*

Morning of 7th September 2020
    Country: Poland. The Bonerowski Palace. Lisa Forrester is having an early morning breakfast served to her in bed, an array of daily newspapers printed in both Polish and English are laid out on one of the bedside tables. Reading through one, a headline catches her eye, it reads 'Chapel Murder'. Curiosity gets the better of her and she begins to read the article.
    CHAPEL MURDER
    British Celebrant Peter North was murdered whilst officiating at a funeral service in Wichita Kansas USA.
    Lisa cries out. 'What! Oh no! Peter.'

It is believed the perpetrator, Sinclair Hopper, took revenge on Celebrant Peter North for defrauding his mother, recently widowed Mrs Bertha Hopper, to the sum of $270,000. This resulted in the homestead being repossessed by the bank. Sinclair Hopper was arrested at the scene and was later charged with homicide.

She folds the newspaper, pauses then rests it on her lap. Picking up her coffee she takes a sip, then smiles.

'Peter, Peter, Peter, such a love.'

*

England. Evening of the 6th September 2020.

On her way out of her office at the SCD9 Unit, DI Fay Guilford spots a headline on a newspaper lying on top of one of her colleague's desk. She stops to read it. With mixed feelings she stands, for a few seconds in thought then unceremoniously drops the newspaper into the office paper recycling bin as she shuts down the lights and closes the door behind her.

At the same time, sitting behind her desk at the Cold Case Fraud Unit, DI Helen Smyth, is handed a newspaper, attached is a yellow post-it note, it reads, *'Article. Pg7 Tony Elms'.* Thumbing through the newspaper she stops at the given page. She rises from her seat, as she reads the article 'Chapel Murder'. After standing in disbelief and with a hint of satisfaction she retrieves Peter North's case file and rubber stamps it 'Case Closed'. Screwing up the newspaper she dropkicks it into the paper recycle bin.

The End

Made in the USA
Columbia, SC
10 June 2022

61575876R00104